LITTLE PEOPLE

BY

PROFESSOR PAUL GRIFFITHS

Interior Design by Booknook.biz.

Table of Contents

Tuesday 29 September 2020

Painter was bored stiff by the perpetual paperwork pile. What he needed was a juicy murder to stimulate the creative side of his thought processes. He stared at the phone on his desk, but the instrument simply stated the time to be 09:15 while sullenly staying silent.

At 09:29 he was startled by a ringing tone on his mobile and a smile passed involuntarily across his face as his brain recognised the name on the screen. A coroner's case could cause those routine files to be relegated to the back burner, so he punched the green button on his iPhone to find out if he was about to be rescued from tedium:

Frederick Butterworth

"Hello Fred; are you still enjoying your post-retirement job?"

"Yes, I am Bill and I'll advise you to consider it when your time comes. It's mostly routine; making sure the bureaucracy runs as smoothly as possible, advising doctors unfamiliar with the system and keeping relatives up to date with progress in complex cases. Then, from time to time, we have the excitement of a suspicious death and I get to talk to my old colleagues again."

"Sounds intriguing. Life here's boring at the moment, so make my day."

"An intensive care Consultant just phoned me to say that he can't issue a death certificate for one of his patients because the death was unexpected, he doesn't know the cause of death and suspects poisoning. I'll text you all the contact details now but thought I'd give you one more piece of information over the phone; the deceased is a VIP, so mind how you go."

* * *

Painter looked up at the tall building with morning autumn sunlight reflecting from the pale blue colour of its gleaming glass exterior. It wasn't really an architectural style he favoured, but it oozed modernity, cleanliness and efficiency. He followed the signs to a lift that took him to the third floor where, as arranged, he dialled a number on his iPhone. As he waited, sounds of beeping and clicking and whirring came to him faintly through the walls. The effect was soporific until the doors were flung open and a dark-haired tall man wearing glasses, white coat and with a stethoscope round his neck strode forward. No detective skills would be needed to ascertain the man's occupation.

"Inspector Painter, I presume; apologies for keeping you waiting and welcome to the Critical Care Department at UCLH. Come this way and I'll tell you what I know about the case."

Painter followed him to a tiny room crammed with four bright red plastic chairs surrounding a miniscule table and tried to keep up with the medical jargon:

"He was in shock when he arrived, so we started standard resuscitation. He had blood-stained vomit, obvious blood in diarrhoea as well as microscopic blood in urine. His initial test results showed a metabolic acidosis, leucocytosis, severely raised liver function tests and raised creatinine showing the kidneys had been damaged as well. This constellation of symptoms and signs is unlike any natural medical disease I've seen before, so I suspected poisoning. I sent samples to our lab and telephoned the National Poisons Information Service. Toxicology results are not back yet from their lab in Birmingham but are expected soon. The patient was obviously severely affected and ventilation was difficult because of obesity, so it was not surprising he did badly, despite our best attempts. I phoned the Coroner's Officer for advice and here you are."

"Did you send the samples under chain of custody?"

"Yes, the Consultant Toxicologist I spoke to gave me the instructions and I followed them to the letter for both urine and faeces. I created a paper form to list each sample with the time taken and the patient's name. I made sure I signed each specimen bottle as well as the paper form itself."

"That's perfect. Please text me the toxicologist's contact details now. When he phones you with a result, ask him to call me as soon as possible. I need to know what we're dealing with here; is it recreational drug use gone wrong; is it accidental poisoning; is it something more sinister?"

* * *

During the ride on the Northern line tube back to New Scotland Yard, Painter thought through his next steps and how he would deploy his new Sergeant. He'd only just got used to the last one when she'd been whisked away to be replaced by another fresh-faced female with limited practical experience and no knowledge of London, having been recruited from the Devon and Cornwall Constabulary. He thought back to yesterday when Veronica told Painter that she expected him to be actively involved in training this new recruit, whose name was Pippa Trelawny. Painter had glanced at the young girl and bit his tongue while wondering silently if the Met was now running a bring your child to work scheme. Trainees can now be accepted from the age of 17 and be out on the streets, under supervision, after just 10 weeks of classroom training, so many now looked ridiculously young to Painter. Pippa had been to university of course; with a degree in English Literature this time. What possible use could that training be to the Metropolitan Police? This fast-track graduate entry scheme was political correctness gone mad. In his opinion, women police officers should focus on what they did best; comforting grieving relatives and making frequent cups of tea for senior male officers. He continued ruminating about these long-term grievances and grumbled to himself as he entered the building and located his team.

"Right, everyone; it looks like we might be dealing with a case of poisoning. As you know, the most common cause is what's called recreational drug use, but I somehow doubt that our 60-something gentleman has been involved in that. The next most common category is poisoning with a household cleaning product. We need to consider this when we go to inspect his house, but most victims are children, not men close to getting their pension. The last category is deliberate poisoning as made famous by Agatha Christie. Before we get carried away with relatives killing our victim with strychnine to claim an inheritance, we need to do some solid, plodding police procedural work. We've no scene of crime as such and so will visit all the places the victim went to on his last day on this planet. Pippa, I told you yesterday that I like all my officers to use public transport where possible. I've already been on the Northern line twice today and we can now all three get on the Bakerloo line for a non-stop trip to our next destination."

Painter didn't want to discuss the case during the journey, so instead took the hint about his responsibility for training and told the girl from Devon and Cornwall about the background to his travel policy.

"The tube system in London is remarkably efficient and compares favourably with the time taken to travel in a squad car through all the dense traffic, even with the siren blaring and blue lights flashing. It also allows us to walk the last portion of our journey to see the built environment where suspects or witnesses live. Does the local architecture raise their spirits when they come home, or does it depress them? Putting your feet on their ground is better than swooping into their life using a squealing squad car. My policy also pleases the Met bean counters who have to sign off on travel expenses. The only disadvantage is that there's no Wi-Fi on the tube so, when we come out of the station, you'll see me check for any urgent messages left on my phone. If you're ever waiting for a reply from me, I'm probably underground."

They came out at Baker Street station and turned to walk towards Madame Tussaud's.

"Here you are; what did I tell you. One voice mail message."

Pippa and Nick stood in silence while Painter returned the call and then wrote brief notes before he turned to them.

"In summary, the toxicologist has a result for us. He

found evidence in both the urine and stool of our victim of a poison called ricin, that comes from castor beans. He looked for the DNA of the poisonous plant in stool but didn't find any. Apparently, that's unusual. If someone accidentally ate some of the beans that contain the poison, both tests should be positive. He's going to repeat all the tests to make sure but says the most likely explanation is that someone extracted and purified the toxin before administering it. Given the symptoms of bloody vomit and diarrhoea, he thinks it was administered by mouth. A large dose would take effect within minutes or hours, a low dose could take half a day. All this new information means that we're definitely dealing with a case of deliberate poisoning and must consider everyone we're about to meet as a potential suspect. Nick: arrange for forensics to send a team straightaway to check the house, particularly the kitchen and bathroom, in case food or things like toothpaste or mouthwash have been contaminated."

Within two minutes, Painter could encourage them to look up at Ulster Terrace and admire the architecture.

"Isn't this glorious? It's a classical design by John Nash, painted in the typical clotted cream colour. The apartments here cost a fortune, so we've got to mind our Ps and Qs, especially as our victim was a knight of the realm."

Painter located the correct number in the terrace and rang the bell. The door was answered by a plump, squat white-haired lady aged about 65 wearing a floral apron.

"I'm Inspector Bill Painter from the Metropolitan Police. I telephoned earlier to arrange to see her ladyship."

"That's right, dear; I took the message when you called. She's expecting you."

Painter, Winters and the new Sergeant followed the woman as she waddled into a large hallway.

"How's she coping?" asked Painter.

"It hasn't really hit her yet, dear, so she's alright at the moment. A bit confused perhaps, but she should be able to answer your questions."

They followed the woman through a doorway into an enormous drawing room, full of light cascading through the large windows that looked out over Regent's Park. He noted the plush curtains, the occasional table standing on a polished wooden floor, Chinese rugs and several large oil paintings with gilt frames, one of which depicted stables with a magnificent horse in the foreground (was it by Stubbs?). A mahogany sideboard had several photographs in silver frames revealing serial old-fashioned pictures of a male and then a female child, each well dressed, sitting in formal poses on the padded upholstery of their comfortably well-off families. Painter took these to be the couple who lived here and noted that there were no modern photographs of any children. Two four-seater Chesterfield settees dominated the centre of the room from one of which a tall, slender woman aged about 60 stood up to reveal she was wearing a plain but elegant black dress accompanied by a single row of grey pearls around her neck.

Painter wondered what the dowager duchess in Downton Abbey would utter as a stage whisper and a phrase came to mind: **Today is not a time for ostentation, but one has to keep up appearances**.

"I'm so sorry to disturb you at this difficult time, your ladyship, but would be obliged if you could tell me about your husband's movements yesterday."

"Of course; please have a seat and Mrs Perkins will bring us all coffee."

"Let's start at the beginning of the day and work our way forward. What time did you both get up yesterday morning?"

"We listened to the morning news on Radio 4, had showers and were eating breakfast by about 8:30."

"What did you eat, exactly?"

"We both had muesli, followed by toast and marmalade."

"Where does your food come from?"

"Why, Harrods of course. When we're coming up to town, Mrs Perkins gives them our standard order, so everything's ready when we need it."

"Does that mean that you don't live here all the time?"

"We have an estate in Somerset which is our main home. We keep this place on as a pied-à-terre."

"How often do you come to London?"

"Usually about once a month. I'm on the board of the Royal Opera House and am committed to attend meetings about 4 times a year. My husband is Chairman of Raffles Private Equity and has about 6 meetings a year. He chooses to arrange these at times to fit in with my schedule and we travel up together. Staying for about a week is convenient because it gives us time to fit in an evening of opera and to dine with old friends."

"How do you travel here from Somerset?"

"Albert brings us."

"And who is Albert?"

"The chauffeur, of course."

"Where can I find him to ask some questions?"

"I imagine he's parked just outside the front door; that's where he's always found when we go out."

Mrs Perkins brought in a large cafetière on an elegant tray, poured for everyone, distributed the cups and disappeared without a word.

"Let's go back to yesterday morning. What did you do after breakfast?"

"Albert took my husband to Mayfair for his meeting and then returned to take me to the Royal Academy to see an exhibition. He then brought me back here at about 5 o'clock."

"Did you meet anyone at the exhibition?"

"Yes, I'd arranged to meet an old friend and we strolled around together."

"When did you hear that your husband had been taken ill?"

"Bertie phoned me to say that John had been taken to hospital. I got Albert to take me there immediately, but I wasn't allowed to see him."

"Who is Bertie?"

"He's one of the directors in Raffles and also a life-long friend of my husband's."

"Do you know where your husband was when he was taken ill?"

"Yes, that dreadful restaurant they always go to after board meetings."

"Do you know the name?"

"Yes, I'm afraid I do. It prides itself on serving school meals to grown up men, so styles itself *Refectory*. I ask you; have you ever heard of anything so foolish?"

"Thank you, your ladyship, for all this information. If you could just let me have the telephone numbers and addresses of the friend you met at the Royal Academy, Bertie and the restaurant, I'll not disturb you any further. I'm afraid that a forensics team will be coming today to take samples from this house and I apologise in advance for any inconvenience this may cause."

"Is that really necessary?"

"I'm afraid it is, your ladyship, because it's possible that your husband was poisoned."

"That doesn't surprise me."

The junior officers looked up from their notebooks and then glanced towards Painter who paused and swallowed hard before asking:

"Can you expand on that by telling me why you're not surprised?"

"It's that ridiculous restaurant with its awful stodgy food. I just wish he'd listened to me and stopped going there."

As Mrs Perkins opened the large front door to show them out, she hailed a man polishing the paintwork of a dark blue Rolls Royce Phantom parked outside.

"Albert; Inspector Painter from the Met needs a word with you."

The man stood up, pocketed his yellow cloth and stepped forward to meet the visitors. He was tall, without glasses and was wearing a smart jacket, but not the peaked cap, that central casting would have provided for the archetypal chauffeur. From the name, Painter was expecting an old family retainer, but the man was barely aged 30.

"Can you run through the duties you performed for Sir John and Lady Pilkington yesterday?"

"Yes, sir. At about 9:30 I took Sir John to his office in Mayfair, arriving just after 10 o'clock. I returned here immediately ready to take her ladyship to the Royal Academy at 11 arriving 11:30. I then cleaned and polished the car and had a bite of lunch with Mrs Perkins before returning to the Royal Academy. I collected her ladyship at 16:30 and we were back here around 17:15, having been delayed in the evening traffic. I then had supper with Mrs Perkins and stood ready to collect Sir John when he phoned from the restaurant, but the call never came. I heard later that he'd been taken ill and I drove her ladyship straight away to University College London Hospital. After about an hour, I drove her back here, parked the car in the garage and retired to the servants' quarters."

"Thank you for that clear description, Albert. Did Sir John eat anything during his morning journey to Mayfair?"

"No sir. He would just have eaten breakfast I assume and would shortly be eating lunch."

"Did Sir John not want you to drive him from his office to the restaurant in the evening?"

"No sir. It's only about two streets away so his habit was to walk with his colleagues."

"One last question; you were polishing the car when we came through the door. Have you also cleaned the inside since yesterday morning?"

"Oh yes, sir. There's a lot of time spent hanging around as a chauffeur. We all use that time to keep our cars looking at their best, whether parked here or in the city."

"Exactly what cleaning did you do yesterday?"

"Well sir, while I'm on the street waiting for my people to need my services, I polish the paintwork with this cloth; always assuming it's not drizzling, because then I use a chamois. When I bring the car back here, I deliver passengers to the front door and then take the car round to the garage at the rear. I use a vacuum cleaner to pick up any pieces of dust and use a different cloth to polish the windows and walnut fittings."

Albert opened the rear near side door of the saloon to allow the visitors to inspect his handiwork. The beige leather of the seats complemented the dark blue paintwork perfectly.

"Excellent work," commented Painter to Albert, before turning to his colleagues:

"Despite the fact that this car has been valeted we'll still get the forensics people to have a look. Now, we must be off to the restaurant where Sir John ate his last meal."

"Would you like me to drive you all there, sir?"

Painter looked at Pippa's eager face before declining the offer.

"That's very kind of you, Albert, but we'll make our own way on the Jubilee line; it's only one stop."

Nobody spoke again until they were well out of the chauffeur's earshot:

"That was a shame, sir; I've never been in a roller," said Pippa.

"Neither have I," replied Painter, "but we need to

be aware that everything we see may be part of a crime scene. What if his wife gave him a special sandwich to eat during the journey that she'd poisoned with ricin? When the forensics report on the car was disclosed to the court revealing traces of the toxin it would have to say that our fingerprints were also found. Can you imagine what a barrister for the defence would say to discredit us in the eyes of the jury: **are you accustomed, Inspector to travelling across London in a Rolls Royce?** No, these folks live in another world and it's the London Underground for the likes of us; we're just the little people."

They had to run down the stairs at Baker Street to catch the southbound train they could hear rattling into the station. After just one stop, Painter could survey the shops in Bond Street and inform his junior colleagues smugly that the heavy traffic would have made the journey by Rolls Royce much longer. Within 5 more minutes they had located the street in Mayfair and then the shop number with the name painted in italics above the doorway; *Refectory*.

Painter showed his warrant card, asked to see the manager and was ushered by a waitress to a corner table. While waiting, he scanned through the menu to see that they did, indeed, offer school meals, just as Lady Pilkington had said, although she hadn't mentioned the exorbitant prices. Painter was particularly impressed by the desserts; bread-and-butter pudding; apple crumble with custard; Eton mess. A tall, trim man aged about 40 appeared and spoke to Painter in an Italian accent:

"How can I help you Inspector? My name is Antonio and I'm the manager of *Refectory.*"

"A tragic incident occurred here last night with Sir John Pilkington. I'm investigating his death and wish to explore the possibility that he reacted to something in the food you served."

"Indeed, I was working yesterday and it was a terrible event. It seems that Sir John felt unwell and went to the bathroom. He was discovered there by one of his colleagues who phoned an ambulance. The first I knew was when two paramedics came running into the restaurant."

"Did you retain the food he was eating?"

"Yes, Inspector; it's standard in the catering trade to store dishes for inspection by Environmental Health Officers if a person is taken ill. However, I can assure you that we have the highest standards of hygiene here."

"Thank you; it makes it much easier for us if samples of food have been retained. What exactly did the Pilkington party have to drink and did they start with anything like olives?"

"They started with a bottle of red wine, a rather nice Pauillac, before ordering food. They didn't have any olives or nuts or bread to dip in olive oil, although these were all on our menu. Sir John had a starter of pea soup. He then had toad in the hole with mashed potatoes and gravy as his main course. This was followed by bread-and-butter pudding. They'd finished one bottle of Pauillac and were part way through a second when he was taken ill. I kept the bottles for inspection also."

"Our forensics team will be with you soon and, with the samples you've retained for us, they shouldn't take long. You should be able to open up as normal this evening."

"Thank you. Inspector. I very much doubt if Sir John's problem originated here, but I'm happy to cooperate in any way I can. Please send my condolences to his widow; Sir John has been a regular customer of ours for many years and will be missed."

"Right, everyone; let's head off for Sir John's office."

"I can show you, Inspector. It's very simple; just one street or so away."

Within two minutes the team arrived at a serviced office block with the name *Raffles Private Equity* listed for the fourth floor. The receptionist made a telephone call and a slim, elegant brunette aged about 30 came bounding down the stairs to greet them.

"Inspector Painter? I'm Susie, Sir John's PA. This has all come as a terrible shock to us; do you know what happened to him?"

"Not yet, Miss but, as part of my investigation, I'd like to see the room where you held the board meeting yesterday."

"Of course, Inspector. Please follow me. It's four floors up, so let's take the lift."

The doors opened on the fourth floor to a carpeted corridor with glass fronted offices on both sides followed by an open plan office area. At the end, occupying the entire width of the building, was the Board Room. It had solid walls, a wooden door and oak panelling within. A mahogany table with 8 chairs dominated the room. At one end was a small kitchenette with coffee service, drinks fridge and cupboards containing crockery.

"Please tell me exactly what Sir John ate and drank yesterday."

"The table was set with wine glasses, tumblers and a bottle of mineral water for each person. Sir John preferred carbonated. We used to have side plates so people could help themselves to cakes provided by a local delicatessen, but Lady Pilkington put a stop to those about 6 months ago to help control his weight. No wine was served yesterday; Sir John disapproved of alcohol until all issues on the agenda had been dealt with. At 1 PM we served sandwiches provided by a local delicatessen."

"Were sandwiches plated out for each person?"

"No, we receive a large platter of assorted sandwiches. When it gets to one o'clock, I remove the clingfilm and pass them around for people to help themselves."

"How many different types of sandwiches were on the platter?"

"We always have the same set; roast beef with horseradish sauce; roast pork with apple sauce; cheddar cheese with pickle; tuna and sweetcorn with mayonnaise."

"Do you know which ones Sir John chose?"

"I wasn't paying too much attention, but he usually takes the roast beef and cheese ones."

"Were there any sandwiches left at the end?"

"Yes, quite a few, because the delicatessen always provides a generous amount."

"What happened to them?"

Susie blushed and hesitated before replying:

"I'm embarrassed to say that a few of the office staff helped me to polish them off. We always do this after a board meeting because it seems such a waste otherwise. I hope you won't charge me with stealing food."

"No, Miss; nothing like that, I just need your honest description of what took place. Did the board members eat anything else?"

"Yes, a platter of fruit was passed around the table. Sir John usually takes a bunch of grapes and some segments of mango."

"Did you and your colleagues finish off the fruit that remained?"

"Yes, I'm embarrassed to admit that we did."

"That's alright, Miss; it's a typical perk of office workers. Did the board members eat or drink anything else?"

"I made coffee in a large pot and poured it for everyone when they arrived. Sir John had his with sugar but not milk. I also made tea for everyone at about 3:30; Sir John had his with milk, but no sugar."

"Did you retain any of these food items for us to inspect?"

"No, Inspector; there was no need to because we didn't know that he'd be taken ill. My colleagues and I ate the food as I told you and then I put all of the plates in the dishwasher. I washed the platters by hand and left them to drain. The only items that remain are the bag of ground coffee, the tea bags and the sugar, all stored in air-tight containers, plus the milk."

"Please direct our forensics team to these items when they arrive. Did any of your work colleagues have any adverse effects from eating the food?"

"Not that I've heard and everyone is here in the office today."

"I then have one final question; was anything different yesterday from a normal board meeting?"

Susie thought for a moment before replying:

"No, Inspector; it was all routine. People arrived, said hello, sat in their usual places, went through the agenda, broke for lunch, visited the loo, returned to the agenda then said farewell at about 5:30."

"Were you with them in this room throughout?"

"Yes, Inspector; except when I received the platters of food at the board room door. I also went to the kitchenette to prepare the platters and make the coffee or the tea."

"Did anyone else go into the kitchenette?"

"No, Inspector, definitely not. I was sitting next to Sir John in the middle of the table looking straight at the kitchenette and would have seen anyone who went in there."

"Thank you for your assistance today. I telephoned one of the directors earlier on and asked him to meet me here. His name is Bertie and he discovered that Sir John had been taken ill in the restaurant. Please bring him here as soon as he arrives."

"I've just been texted to say that he's in reception, so I'll go and collect him now. Would you then all like coffee?"

Receiving a grateful set of nods, the PA set off to complete her tasks.

The door to the board room soon opened and in walked a man aged about 65 of average weight and height. What was not average about him was the choice of cloth for his three-piece tailored suit which was made from the boldest brown and yellow check that Painter had ever seen. His black hair was cut so it fell in thick curls to surround his face in a style that would be attractive to women. He was wearing a waspish smile, exuded confidence and gave every appearance of having led an exciting life.

"You must be Bertie; thank you for finding time to meet up with us this afternoon."

"You're welcome, old chap. I live just down the road in Mayfair, so it was no imposition for me."

"Can you start by telling me how you met Sir John?"

"We went to school together; Eton College. He was the bright one; I was just in his shadow academically. But we were great chums and remained in touch when we left school, both training as accountants in London. John moved into private equity then set up his own fund a few years later. He needed a couple of non-executive directors so naturally asked Nigel and me to join the company. He did all the work and we just cast an eye over the acquisitions and sales he was planning."

"Did Nigel go to the same school?"

"Yes, he did; we were all in the same house, actually."

"Is Nigel the third person who went with you to the restaurant last night?"

"Yes, that's right. We make a habit of meeting up like old chums after every board meeting, chatting about people we were at school with and what they're up to now."

"Can you briefly tell us what happened last night?

Bertie's shoulders slumped and his bonhomie faded away in front of their eyes before he took a deep gulp and finally spoke.

"It was the worst evening of my life, Inspector. John was his normal self during the board meeting. He was also

OK to begin with at the restaurant where he had soup, toad in the hole and bread-and-butter pudding. When we were part way through our second bottle of Pauillac he got up to go to the loo but looked a little queasy. This was unlike him; he normally has a hearty appetite, so I was concerned for him. I followed and found him staring into the mirror in the washroom. He looked as white as a sheet, then vomited into the sink. He looked up for a moment but then fell to the ground. I could see blood in the vomit as I dialled 999. The rest all happened in a haze. I crouched next to him and could feel a pulse. He was still breathing. Then the ambulance people rushed in, took over and whisked him away. I was shocked. I remembered to wash my hands before I went back to Nigel. We didn't feel like eating or drinking anything after that. I telephoned his wife and told her that John had been taken to UCLH. I paid the bill and we went our separate ways home. It was so unlike the boisterous, friendly meals that I was used to having with my best friend."

"It sounds like you were closer to Sir John than were the other directors."

"Yes, they had what you might call a face-to-face relationship with him. That is, they always met him across his desk or across the table in the board room. I met him at those same board meetings, but also went out with him to dinner. I also had the privilege of being invited to his home on several occasions."

"It seems that Sir John has had a very successful career."

"Absolutely. He had an eye for the types of businesses we want and almost all of them have been financial successes."

"What types of businesses are they?"

"The thing they have in common is financial distress, but the subjects they deal in are very varied. At the moment we have positions in light industrial, light manufacturing, microbrewery, retail, care homes, bottling plants and paper products."

"That seems a very wide range of areas; how do you manage to stay on top of all of them?"

"I don't; we only need to have an overview of the finances. An ideal company would be family owned with freehold property and a competent manager. They may be losing their way due to lack of investment, too much debt, over-staffing, excess bureaucracy or even the temporary effects of the pandemic. We come in, buy the business and incentivize the manager to improve productivity by getting rid of the dead wood. If he needs a new bit of equipment, we buy it for him. We don't deal with his customers directly so don't interfere with his decisions. This frees up the company to show those animal spirits of enterprise that John Maynard Keynes wrote about so eloquently; the emotional mindsets that drive economic growth. After a year or two the company is usually growing nicely. We next sell the property and lease it back, using the proceeds to pay off any particularly expensive debt. The balance sheet now looks much better, so we pay ourselves a dividend and float the company with an Initial Public Offering. This typically takes 4-5 years from start to finish and yields high returns."

"If you sold the property and leased it back the company must have another debt on its books."

"Yes, but the standard way of accounting for a lease is much more flattering for the accounts than owning property and having a bank loan to pay for it. The new accounts show that we've turned around the business and people are happy to pay good money to get shares in a company with an improving balance sheet. Of course, if interest rates go up the company may find it more difficult to keep up with payments for the lease, but that's no longer our problem. The process has been described as buy, pump and dump. I know that some people call us parasites for doing this, but I'll remind you that those creatures die if their prey dies. It's in the interests of both parasites and private equity to have healthy bodies beneath them."

"Thank you for that memorable description of your work. How much money did Sir John make by following the system you describe?"

"I don't know exactly, but it must be billions. He bought his estate in Somerset and rents that lovely Nash Terrace in Regent's Park."

"That house is rented?"

"Yes, they're all owned by the Crown Estate who provide long leases, typically for 999 years. Of course, it's rented by Raffles Private Equity, not John himself; much more tax-efficient that way."

"What else did he do with his money?"

"He became a major benefactor. The Royal Opera House and Great Ormond Street Hospital for Children initially, but then he decided to provide substantial sums for soldiers and sailors injured while fighting for our country. He committed a lot of time to this and changed from being our Chief Executive to our Chairman, promoting the Chief Finance Officer in the process. John still took the major decisions about the company, but no longer had to deal with the mechanics of the day to day running. It allowed him to spend more time with his other interests and led to him getting his knighthood about 5 years ago for services to charity. His wife was frightfully pleased to be called Your Ladyship."

"That career of cut and thrust finance must have made Sir John a fair few enemies; can you think of any who would wish to see him dead?"

"Quite a lot really. He did out-manoeuvre many in the city."

Painter's stony stare caused Bertie to reconsider.

"Oh, I see; you're being serious. I apologise if I was a bit flippant there. John had lots of rivals in business, but no-one who would really harm him. Why are you asking? Do you think he was killed?"

"There are some indications that he might have been poisoned. Can you think of any business rivals who might have done that?"

Bertie didn't reply immediately.

"Would you mind awfully if I didn't try to answer that question? Your description sounds rather like the Mafia. We're not involved in anything like that. If we lose a target that we've been tracking for a while, that's all part of the game, all part of business. This is an occupation for us, but also an entertainment. None of us is going to starve if we fail to win a target."

"I appreciate it might be distasteful to you, but can I press you to give me an answer?"

"Very well; no, I can't think of anyone we know who would act like the Mafia."

"Well, continue to mull it over and let me know if you think we should look into any particular person. We can do this very discretely and rule them out of consideration without them even knowing that we've been looking. Here's my card if you have any ideas."

Bertie looked troubled as he left the room in less boisterous style than he had entered. Once the door to the board room had closed, Painter gave instructions to his team.

"Let's call it a day for now. We've evidence of poisoning so our next move will be guided by the results of the forensic tests at the various places he visited. While we wait for those scientists to tell us where the deed was done, get the names of the other directors who attended the board meeting and Nick can invite them here to give their formal statements. Tomorrow, come to my office at 08:00. Pippa and I will then go to Regent's Park. Lady Pilkington will expect to see the senior officer, so I'll get her statement while Pippa does the same for Mrs Perkins and Albert. Finally, Pippa; use your university degree to write me a report, no longer than two pages, on the plant that produces castor oil, the seeds, where you can buy them and what their appearance is, to stop us looking foolish if one of these office plants is the thing we're after. While you're doing that, I'll be doing some homework on Private Equity and conducting the formal interview on Bertie, because money's behind many a mischief in my experience."

∞

Wednesday 30 September 2020

At the 8 AM meeting, the recent recruit from Devon and Cornwall Constabulary spoke clearly to impress her new boss:

"Here's a photo of the plant that you requested, sir. But even better than that is an app I found last night. It's for gardeners who fancy the look of something they see in a neighbour's garden or in a garden centre. You point the camera at the plant, press the button and the phone displays the name. It also gives tips on how to cultivate the plant, although that's not our objective today."

"That's great Pippa, I'll download the app now from the Apple store. While we're waiting, it occurs to me that we could use that additional information you mentioned. Type in the name and it should tell us what conditions would have been needed to grow it."

"Good idea, sir. I'll read out what it says. **For best results, sow the seeds of this half hardy annual in good light at any time in early spring into a good soil-based compost. Cover the seeds with fine grit or compost to approximately their own depth. Germination at 15 to 20 degrees centigrade normally takes between 2 and 6 weeks. Pot on the seedlings before finally planting out into a large container to stand on the patio. Alternatively, transfer to a well-drained spot to create a dra-**

matic focal point in beds or borders. Mature plants reach a height of 90-120 cm. They have exotic-looking foliage and flower in the summer. Beware, the seeds are poisonous."

"Well, that's more than enough information to be going on with. Now's the time to head off to our allotted tasks; meet you all back here at 16:00."

The Jubilee line behaved itself so Painter could soon look up at the clotted cream façade and give Pippa a brief history of this part of the capital city that he loved so much:

"John Nash in the early 1800s designed all of these terraces that were built by speculative builders who used the money from the first sales to fund the building of the next set. He worked for the Prince Regent, planned additional freestanding villas in Regent's Park and expected his Regent Street to run all the way down to the Regent's residence, which he rebuilt into Buckingham Palace."

The door was then opened by Mrs Perkins and the two police officers set about getting formal statements from their people with distinct social backgrounds.

"I'll keep the disruption to a minimum, your ladyship; the aim is to document in a formal written statement what you told me yesterday and to see if you've anything to add. I've taken the liberty of producing a draft to save you some time."

Lady Pilkington took out her glasses and read every sentence carefully before looking up:

"That all seems correct to me, Inspector; even if it does sanitise the worst day of my life with its focus on the trivialities of who went where and when. Where would you like me to sign?"

"Now the formal part is over, I have to remind you that we've indications that your husband may have been poisoned. This could've occurred by accident but it's my job to consider whether it may have been deliberate. Can you suggest the names of any people who may have wished your husband harm?"

"Not that I can think of. The whole idea is abominable to me. Everyone who met him loved John. No, Inspector, there's no-one in our social life who would do such a thing. I can't speak for my husband's business acquaintances, so suggest you put your question to Bertie."

"Thank you, your ladyship. One more question if I may which I'm obliged to ask everyone who finds themselves in your position; do you know who will inherit according to your husband's will?"

"Of course I do, Inspector. John and I have mirror wills. We were not blessed with children, so the wills are very straightforward. When the first of us dies, the second has a life interest in everything we own. When I die, there will be a bequest to certain family members with the remainder donated to the two charities we supported: opera and disabled veterans. You can get the full details from our solicitor."

* * *

"Thank you for coming to New Scotland Yard, sir. Can we start by seeing if this draft I've prepared of what you told me yesterday will serve as a formal statement?"

The man in the remarkable suit read every word carefully before replying:

"Yes, that's a correct version of the terrible events."

"Can I then ask if you've had time to consider whether any business competitor might have poisoned your old friend?"

Bertie looked uncomfortable as he shuffled in his seat.

"I feel awful even making this suggestion, but there's one person who might fit the profile you described. I'd never have thought of it myself but, once you put the idea into my brain, I couldn't get rid of it. I've printed out his details on this piece of paper, together with a list of deals where our firm beat his."

He reached into the inside pocket of his extraordinary yellow and brown check jacket and passed over a single sheet of A4 paper.

"Can I have your assurance that I'll never be revealed as the source of any information?"

"Yes, sir; I can give you that assurance."

Painter glanced at the name, raised his eyebrows and looked straight at Bertie.

"I appreciate that he's a household name, but he's always been jealous of John and our fund did beat his to many lucrative targets."

* * *

Painter sat in his office reviewing the formal statements as Nick and Pippa emailed them in. He then answered his phone:

Jim Sadler

"I've done a full post mortem exam on your Sir John. I started by spending a lot of time going over every centimetre of his skin with a hand lens but couldn't find a single puncture point, except the tubes inserted at UCLH for his resuscitation. I can't give you a guarantee but think it's very unlikely he was injected with ricin. This is supported by the extensive haemorrhage in his upper gastrointestinal tract, consistent with ingestion of a toxin. The ricin was absorbed and spread in his bloodstream to damage his kidneys and liver so must have been in his system for many hours. However, some of that absorption would have occurred after he was taken ill."

"I sense you're trying to help me localise the time of day when he was poisoned."

"That's correct, but it's more difficult than usual because the levels of toxins in tissues and blood can't be related to a large database of prior cases. Very few people have been poisoned with ricin, so I don't think the levels, when they come back from the toxicology lab, will be able to add much to what I saw with my own eyes once I'd opened him up. Formally, my written report will say that the toxic effects are consistent with a low dose at breakfast, a medium dose at lunch or a high dose at dinner. However, just between you and me, I'd suggest that contamination of his dinner would have to have used a very high dose, so is less likely. It would also be easier to detect remaining traces at the scene if a large dose was used. Conversely, that does mean that a small dose given at breakfast would be the most difficult to detect, especially as the person responsible would have several hours to clean up afterwards."

"Thanks Jim, that's just the type of guidance I need about where to focus on next. Would the ricin have given the food a strange taste?"

"I imagine not, because he didn't refuse the food it was disguised with. However, I can't be sure because, as you'll appreciate, the few people poisoned with ricin can't tell us much about it."

* * *

The junior officers arrived punctually for the 4 PM meeting.

"I've been reading your reports as they came in. All the witness statements agree with each other and helped me to create the timeline on the whiteboard."

All eyes swivelled to watch as Painter took them through the events of the fateful day.

"We know that Sir John ate breakfast with his wife around 8:30. This is corroborated by Mrs Perkins who agrees that they both ate muesli, followed by toast and marmalade. We know that Albert took him at 9:30 to Mayfair arriving at his office just after 10 o'clock. This is corroborated by Susie, his PA. We know that all board members drank coffee before and during the first session of the meeting; they all corroborate that. Sir John had black coffee with sugar. He also drank some carbonated water from a bottle left at his place. We know Sir John ate sandwiches at 1 PM. The PA believes he selected roast beef and cheese, but no-one else noticed his choice. All the sandwiches were eaten by the board members or the clerical staff afterwards so, if a poisoned sandwich was used to kill him, it must have been a single one targeted at him in some way. A second platter contained fruit; Susie thinks he had grapes and mango, but no-one else noticed. We know that all board members had a comfort break after lunch and before resuming the meeting; two people remember seeing Sir John at the urinals, so that excludes the possibility of him hiding himself in a stall to take what he thought was a recreational drug. They all had afternoon tea at 3:30 and the meeting ended amicably at 5:30. All the food taken in the board room was delivered from a delicatessen on platters and passed around for people to help themselves. These platters and all the drinks were prepared in the kitchenette by Susie and she's adamant that no-one else went into that room. The board members are a bit vague about this because it wasn't their responsibility I suppose, but we can say that none of them saw anyone other than Susie go into the kitchenette. By 6 PM, three of them, Sir John, Bertie and Nigel, were in the restaurant, having taken barely 5 minutes to walk there. They took their time over dinner. The manager, Antonio, told us that they started with wine. No tasty morsels like olives or peanuts were consumed. They ordered their food and the first course arrived just before 7 PM. Sir John had pea soup. There was then a gap before his toad in the hole was served. At this point they started their second bottle of red wine. For dessert, Sir John had bread-and-butter pudding. All his meal choices were corroborated by Bertie and by Nigel. Sir John ate all of his food without complaining of any strange tastes. Around 8:15 he said he was feeling queasy, went to the washroom, vomited, collapsed and was taken to hospital. His wife visited at 10 PM but he was too sick to be seen. He was certified dead at 3 AM. Now, have I left anything out?"

"No sir, except to say that it's difficult to see how someone could have slipped him the poison."

"I agree, Nick. The only thing specifically earmarked for him was carbonated water left at his place at the head of the table, but it was in a glass bottle with a seal, so he would presumably have rejected it if the seal was broken. Fortunately, we should receive the results of the forensic sampling of each site before 1 PM tomorrow. Meet me here at noon and we'll go through any new things we find. Pippa, go to his solicitor and get a copy of his will to see if it says exactly what Lady Pilkington told me. Nick, check out this person on the police computer but be discrete. There's a list of deals where Sir John's fund beat his company. I want to know if this business rivalry with Sir John could have led this man to murder, but I don't want anyone to know that we're considering this possibility. Also, make a list of all the companies owned by Raffles Private Equity and search the press and social media for any stories of people falling out with Bertie and his colleagues. I'd be particularly interested in an owner or shareholder in a small company who felt they'd been shafted and threatened retribution. My background reading about private equity confirms my belief that they're more interested in restructuring the finances of a company than in helping them make real increases in productivity or improving the long-term viability of the company. Their focus on financial engineering is risky with companies going bust if interest rates rise. By then, the private equity whiz kids may have sold up and moved on leaving some gullible investor holding the now bankrupt company. I couldn't blame that person for feeling angry under these circumstances."

Thursday 1 October 2020

The detective constable gave his results first.

"I went through the links to the press stories you gave me. This man does indeed have a long-standing rivalry with Sir John and lost several high-profile bids for companies. Although that could, in theory, give him a motive for murder, the police national computer has no adverse comments about him; not even a speeding ticket. He also has no listed suspicious contacts with known criminals."

"Thanks Nick. He's a plausible candidate but wouldn't do the dirty himself; he'd employ a hit man. Let's leave him on hold until we know which venue was used. When we get leads, remain alert to the possibility they may be connected to him. What about you, Pippa; what have you got to tell us?"

"Well, sir. I checked with the solicitor and Sir John's will is exactly as his wife told you. I asked the solicitor if he was not surprised that Sir John had not wanted to do more to avoid inheritance tax, but he told me that his client was happy to pay this as a way of recycling the wealth he created back into society. The solicitor also pointed out that the rate of inheritance tax would be reduced from 40% to 36% because of the substantial donation to charity."

"Thanks Pippa. I think that's all the loose ends tied up now. We just need to wait for this phone to ring."

Just as a watched kettle never seems to boil, Painter's iPhone stayed stubbornly silent. The trio busied themselves with trivial items until, despite knowing that it was coming, all three jumped when the ringing tone shattered the silence.

"Hold on a moment; I'll put you on speakerphone. Ok now. I'm in my office with Sergeant Pippa Trelawny and Detective Constable Nick Winters so you can speak freely. We're all waiting to hear which site was the source of the poison."

"That's just it, Inspector; all our tests gave a blank. Completely negative; not even a trace. I'll run them all again to be sure, but all the positive controls worked and the sensitivity of the assay is excellent so I think you have to consider that no open source of toxin was present at those sites."

"What exactly do you mean by open source?"

"If anyone prepared the toxin from the beans in any room we sampled, I'm confident we'd have found it. If toxin was poured from a bottle into someone's drink, I'd have expected to detect at least traces. These are both examples of open sources where minute droplets can contaminate surfaces. In contrast, a closed source has been prepared elsewhere, wiped clean and taken away from the contaminated environment. Crucially, it mustn't be opened at the site of the crime."

"What about a bottle of carbonated drinking water?" asked Painter.

"It's only a closed source until it's opened. Unscrewing the bottle and pouring it out would produce contamination."

"Well, what type of closed source would work for our situation?"

"Someone could prepare ricin and use a needle and syringe to infiltrate the sausages incorporated into the toad in the hole eaten by the victim. This would produce contamination where the drug was inoculated but not in the kitchen where the sausages were cooked, which was one of the places we sampled. However, cooking at a high temperature would destroy ricin quickly. Alternatively, a medicine capsule would do. The capsules could be prepared elsewhere, cleaned and moved to the scene of the crime. The capsule's swallowed whole and only releases its contents once inside the body of the recipient. The capsule could be given as itself or disguised within a food item; preferably one that's not cooked."

"Ok; I can see those as real-world examples. How long would ricin be stable for at room temperature if it wasn't cooked?"

"Oh, months and months."

"Thank you for all of this. It wasn't the message I

thought I was going to receive today, but it's given us plenty of, shall we say, food for thought."

Painter ended the call and turned towards his two junior colleagues.

"I wasn't expecting that at all. This will need some serious thinking, so I suggest I buy you both a milky coffee."

Pippa gave Nick a quick glance and the pair smiled at this unusual display of generosity from their notoriously grumpy boss.

He took them to the cafe on the ground floor of the Westminster tube refurbishment, across from the Palace of Westminster. They then carried their drinks as they followed him to a part of the Embankment devoid of passers-by where they could speak freely.

"We need to work through this logically. When he woke up on his last day alive, who was the first person Sir John saw who could hurt him?"

"His wife, sir."

"She was the second person, Pippa; the first was himself."

Pippa looked surprised for a moment then asked:

"Are you suggesting he committed suicide?"

"Why not? We've clearly got a mystery on our hands with no obvious suspect. The poison was prepared elsewhere as part of a premeditated plan; perhaps Sir John designed it himself."

"But we've no evidence that he was contemplating suicide."

"Exactly; that's one new direction our investigations now need to take us. I'll interview her ladyship and ask, discretely, about his state of mind."

Painter took a sip of his cappuccino, which he'd ordered with low fat milk in deference to his GP's guidance to lose weight before saying:

"Now we can turn to his wife as the second person he saw. When I interview her, I'll try to get an idea about the state of her marriage. Pippa, go back and see Sir John's solicitor and approach the same subject. Had they ever considered divorce or consulted him about dividing their financial assets? Nick, go and interview the woman who her ladyship says she spent the afternoon with at the Royal Academy. As well as confirming her story, find out if they had a happy marriage."

Painter took another sip of his drink before continuing:

"We then turn to the third person he saw that morning, Mrs Perkins. I'll interview her while I'm at Regent's Park. I'll do the same for the fourth person; Albert the chauffeur. The fifth person to see him was Susie, the PA. Go there again Pippa and see if she acts defensively. Meanwhile I'll talk to the sixth person, Bertie, while Nick goes to see Antonio and gets the details of the waitress who served their table as well as information about the sausages used in the toad in the hole. Then, divide all the suspects up between you and do financial checks on all of them. I'm wondering if someone, perhaps the well-known head of the rival private equity fund, paid one of them to trick Sir John into swallowing food containing the poison. Let's meet back at my office at 15:00 tomorrow to discuss all these results."

Friday 2 October 2020

The sky was grey, with humidity in the air presaging archetypal British drizzle as Painter walked to his destination. The front elevation of the terrace was still in shadow, but he could imagine how spectacular the clotted cream colour would appear once the sun had passed overhead. The door was answered by Mrs Perkins and he found himself invited to sit once again on the comfortable Chesterfield.

"I'm sorry to disturb you today your ladyship but have some further questions for you."

Receiving neither disapproval nor encouragement he continued:

"May I see the medicines that Sir John took on that fateful morning?"

"If you wish. Mrs Perkins will fetch them now."

Appearing slightly flustered by this turn of events, Mrs Perkins set down the tray containing the freshly brewed cafetière and waddled away.

"He always kept them by his bedside, so this should only take a moment or two."

The housekeeper returned with a screw-capped jar containing capsules labelled valsartan that were half blue and half yellow.

"Thank you; may I take these away?"

"Of course you may; they are of no use to me now."

"Can I ask which doctor prescribed them for Sir John and the address of the surgery?"

"Why, Harley Street, of course. I'll give you the full details."

Mrs Perkins completed the task of dispensing coffee and withdrew.

"Can I then ask a more delicate question, your ladyship. We know that Sir John was poisoned. Is there any possibility that he could have planned this himself, as a way of taking his own life?"

Lady Pilkington exerted pressure on the back of the Chesterfield as she drew herself into her most upright position:

"My husband was not a coward, Inspector. He would never have committed suicide under any circumstances. He also had no reason to commit such an act, being in good health. Finally, he had a sunny disposition which I understand to be the opposite of the type of personality he would need if your proposition were to be true. Thus, I conclude that there is no possibility whatsoever that my husband died at his own hand."

Painter felt the coffee burning his gullet but needed to drain the cup and make his escape.

"Thank you, your ladyship, for answering my questions and I apologise again for having to ask them to exclude even remote possibilities from my enquiry. With your permission I'll now interview Mrs Parsons and Albert again briefly before leaving you in peace."

Painter managed to keep the interviews with Mrs Perkins and with Albert short and to the point. He came out of the fabulous house to find the sun trying to break through the thin clouds with flashes of sunlight reflected from the many small puddles from the light rain that he'd been spared. He had time to walk briskly to Harley Street and would then still make the later appointment he'd arranged with Bertie.

The doctor was in his clinic, but not pleased to be disturbed.

"I can spare you 5 minutes only, Inspector, although I can tell you that I know nothing about the sudden death of Sir John."

"Did he have a serious illness?"

"No. He was overweight and had hypertension, but nothing immediately life threatening."

"Is it possible he was depressed and so might take his own life?"

"He had no history of depression. One can never be sure, but he was the least likely person to commit suicide in my opinion."

"Do you know if he considered his marriage to be a happy one?"

"I wouldn't really know, but he never gave any indication of a problem in that direction."

"Can you confirm that you prescribed this medicine for him?" asked Painter, showing the bottle of valsartan capsules.

"Yes, I think so," replied the doctor, "although I'd want to check my records to be sure."

"I imagine that you gave him a prescription, but do you know which chemist actually dispensed the medicines?"

The doctor's face produced a thin, sardonic smile.

"I fear you don't quite appreciate the standard of medical service we provide to the very busy patients who come to us here in Harley Street. I write a prescription, call my receptionist, give her the prescription form and explain to the patient that the medicines will arrive promptly if they will just have a seat in our comfortable waiting room. While my receptionist runs round to the dispensary, which serves a series of clinics in Harley Street, the patients enjoy a cup of coffee and a read of *Tatler*, or *Vogue* perhaps, while waiting. I'm sure today's receptionist will be able to give you all the details you need."

With that, Painter was ushered from the presence of the ever-so-important doctor and into the arms of the more helpful Trudy.

"Oh yes, I remember Sir John. Such a shame to hear what happened to him. Let me check his record. Here it is; I took the prescription round to the dispensary myself and will take you there now."

Painter followed as she descended to the basement and took a long connecting corridor before entering a large room with a tabletop providing a barrier to a workspace with shelves studded with enormous bottles of coloured tablets and capsules on the wall behind. She introduced him to the head pharmacist and was free to leave once she'd given Painter her contact details.

Painter learned that the tablets and capsules were dispensed in what was described as the traditional method. He watched as a junior pharmacist poured tablets from a large bottle onto a triangular flat plate with raised edges and tipped it gently to see if they reached a mark on the metal. She returned 3 tablets to the large bottle and lifted the triangular plate so that the remaining tablets slid into a small screw-topped bottle. She added a label from the printer and put the tablets on top of the counter. The head pharmacist checked the prescription and the label on the bottle, initialled the prescription form, separated the two identical parts of the form and gave the top copy plus the tablets to a waiting receptionist.

"You see, this all works very efficiently. We serve 6 practices here in Harley Street and are familiar with all the medicines that our doctors are likely to prescribe."

"What happens to the lower copy of the prescription form?"

"It's scanned overnight for our records thereby generating an invoice for the practice and the list that we need to submit to our accountant. We're fully computerised now."

Painter looked up at the row of outsized glass jars that would have been familiar to Samuel Pepys and asked diplomatically:

"Does that mean that your computer can tell me who exactly dispensed the last set of tablets that were given to Sir John?"

"It can indeed if you just bear with me a moment. Yes, here we are; the tablets and capsules were dispensed by Fiona, who you just observed working, and approved by me."

Painter spoke to Fiona to obtain her contact details.

"Is there anything else I can help you with?" asked the head pharmacist.

"Yes, there is. How many other patients in your 6 practices have been prescribed those capsules recently?"

The head pharmacist fought with the computer before answering:

"Four other patients, Inspector."

"Can you print off their names and addresses please?"

"I can't do that because patients attend here under medical confidentiality."

"I'm aware of that and will protect their identities but I'm conducting a murder enquiry."

The woman looked uncertain about what to do until Painter added:

"I could get a warrant if you prefer, but it would mean closing down the pharmacy for several hours."

He was soon guided out of the building while safely clutching an A4 piece of printer paper bearing details of the 4 patients.

Painter got his bearings and set off on a brisk walk to Mayfair. He was only 3 minutes late on arrival but felt the need to apologise.

"Thank you for seeing me again. I'm sorry to be running a bit behind schedule today."

"No problem at all, Inspector," replied Bertie. "Have a seat and some coffee."

"I need to ask you two delicate questions. First, do you think it possible that Sir John could have given himself the poison as a way of committing suicide?"

After a few moments, Bertie burst into laughter.

"Not a chance, Inspector. John enjoyed life and lived it to the full, both in his work and in recreation. Someone less likely to get depressed and commit suicide would be difficult to find."

"That's a clear enough answer to that question, thank you. I wonder what you'll say to the second. Did Sir John and Lady Pilkington have a happy marriage?"

Bertie was pensive before replying.

"Yes, I'd say that they were happy. I know they regretted not having children but had filled their life together by planning trips to the opera and going on extravagant holidays. He knew he was declining in the way that trees drop their leaves as autumn appears, but he hadn't reached the stage of having bare branches yet. He was managing his ageing by giving up being CEO and moving on to chair the successful business he'd created. He had his work to occupy him and had latterly moved to develop an intense interest in his charities. She loved being on the Board of the Royal Opera House at Covent Garden. I never got the slightest inclination that they weren't a happy couple."

Painter left the Mayfair flat and hurried towards the tube to get back to his office for his 15:00 meeting with Nick and Pippa. He was annoyed to be held up at a crossing, but the lights soon changed and the crowd of tourists surged forward sweeping him along. He wondered if he should stop and get a sandwich for lunch on the go, but hated eating in public, including on the tube, except for ice cream cones that seemed designed to be flaunted. As if on cue, a shop selling Italian ice cream appeared. It was ridiculously expensive, but this was Mayfair after all. He selected two of his favourites; vanilla topped with a scoop of rum and raisin. He walked out of the shop and made his way gingerly lest the exorbitant treat ended up on the pavement. Once the cone had been devoured in its entirety, he stopped by a glass fronted shop to check that his face was wiped clean of incriminating clues and quickened his pace, eventually reaching New Scotland Yard exactly on time.

"Right then; let's go through all the people in order, starting with Sir John. I'll kick off. I got these capsules of valsartan from his wife and will get them tested to see if they've been poisoned. I also asked his widow and his doctor and then Bertie if Sir John might have committed suicide and got a definite no from all three of them. What did you find out about the background finances?"

"It's really complicated, sir, said Pippa, "but they promise to let us have a summary by tomorrow lunch-time. However, I did find out from Susie how much the private equity fund pays to rent their house in Regent's Park. It's £16,000 per month."

"That's ridiculous," said Nick.

"I'll remind you that Bertie told us earlier that it was a tax-deductible expense, so its honest taxpayers like you and me who're paying for it. The little people always end up getting screwed. Turning now to Lady Pilkington, I asked their doctor in Harley Street about them and he assumed they were happily married. The same goes for Bertie, who would know them even better."

"I asked the solicitor the same question and got the same reply, sir," said Pippa.

"We now have one new person to insert in our sequence. I asked the doctor where Sir John's medicines came from and it turns out that Harley Street has its own dispensary. I went there and got these details of Fiona, a junior pharmacist, who counted out his capsules. I'll add her to the whiteboard and she needs a financial check, please. I next interviewed Mrs Perkins. She seemed very straightforward and has a good reason not to want to see her employer die. She's a widow and lives very comfortably in Somerset with regular trips in a Rolls Royce to London. Did her financial check reveal anything?"

"Nothing unusual, sir. She's a small amount of savings but hasn't received any large sums recently."

"The same goes for Albert. His hours have to be flexible to fit in with the exotic lifestyle, but he's happy with staff accommodation in Somerset and Regent's Park. He's not married and gives the appearance of being settled into a comfortable life. He also gets to drive a Rolls Royce. He wouldn't want to see his employer die."

"His financial check was clean, sir. A small amount of money in a cash ISA but no recent influx of a large sum."

"Thanks Nick. That takes us to Susie, the PA; what did you find out, Pippa?"

"Well sir; I had a good long chat with her. She wasn't defensive, as if she were hiding something, and seemed genuinely upset at Sir John's death. I came back to the office to find a clean financial check for her too."

"Next on our list is Bertie. I've seen him several times now and believe he's genuinely sad to see his old friend die. I doubt if he killed Sir John."

"There's no recent receipt of a large sum of money, sir, but he has regular payments from several sources and owns loads of shares in companies. He also owns his flat in Mayfair without a mortgage; current value of the property is 2.8 million."

"That's what we'd expect for a director in a private equity fund and also illustrates that a bribe would be unlikely to persuade him to help kill his friend. That leads us on to Antonio, the manager of the restaurant; what did you find out, Nick?"

"He told me that they receive many sausages twice a week and cook them at 250 degrees centigrade when making toad in the hole. There are no sausages remaining from the batch used to make Sir John's meal. Antonio seemed a genuine person and wasn't anxious about being interviewed again. His financial check also didn't reveal anything. However, he did locate for me the waitress who served Sir John that night. She was nervous when I interviewed her, so I assume you'd like us to do a financial check on her as well?"

"Yes please. In summary, we've no suggestion of any real leads so far, but it's early days in this investigation. Complete all those financial checks and then request full background checks on everyone, before meeting tomorrow in my office at 13:00. That includes this list of 4 other people that I'm adding to the whiteboard."

"Who are they, sir?"

"They're the only other people that the pharmacy in Harley Street supplies with the same capsules. I'm wondering if the target wasn't Sir John, but one of them instead and someone made a mistake and slipped the poisoned capsule into the wrong screw-capped medicine bottle."

∞

Saturday 3 October 2020

Painter was pleased that both of his junior officers turned up on time for the 1 PM meeting but didn't bother to tell them; praise wasn't his style.

"Let's catch up with things left over from yesterday and then I'll tell you how I spent this morning. Who's got the financial report on Sir John?"

"I have, sir," said Pippa. "It's really complicated because he has money in so many places. Large sums come and go into the Raffles fund as we might expect, but no new sources of money have appeared recently. His personal wealth can only be described as fabulous. He has shares in loads of companies that are managed by a stockbroker. His personal accounts are much easier to follow. He has several large sums deposited as fixed term bonds with a series of banks. His current account is always in balance with at least £10,000. He has two credit cards, each platinum, that pay off the debt automatically at the end of each month. He has separate current and savings accounts with a local bank in Somerset that deals with all transactions related to his estate down there. I looked to see if there were any suspicious regular payments that might represent blackmail but couldn't see any. However, the whole financial setup is really complex so I couldn't guarantee that everything's kosher."

"That'll have to do as a first look at our victim. Now let's turn to potential perpetrators who I suspect will have much more modest means. Next on our list is Fiona, the trainee pharmacist."

"I looked into her finances, sir," volunteered Nick. "She has the typical profile of a young professional. Student loan from her time studying pharmacy at Nottingham University. Modest salary from the dispensary at Harley Street. Regular payments for a house share in Notting Hill. She has a positive balance on her current account each month, but it's a fraction of what Sir John has. She's never actually been overdrawn but sails close to the wind on some months. There are no unusual recent payments into her account. I also looked into the finances of the waitress at the restaurant. She's in an even worse financial position. She lives with a boyfriend in Maida Vale in a one-bedroom basement flat. She uses her overdraft every month and sometimes risks exceeding the allowance. She's not had a recent influx of a suspicious large sum of money. In summary, both of these young women could potentially have had their heads turned by the offer of money, but don't appear to have received any. Neither of them has a record on the police national database. I've requested full background checks on both of them."

"Thanks Nick. It doesn't look like either of them was bribed to poison Sir John, but we'll keep an open mind. What about the 4 new names I gave you yesterday?"

"We each took two of them, sir. I'll add all the details to the whiteboard but, in summary, there's nothing that stands out as being suspicious. All 4 of them are between 60 and 68 years of age, which isn't surprising for people with blood pressure problems. They all had health insurance provided by their employers which is how they came to be seen at Harley Street. Two of them have since retired but elected to continue paying for health insurance out of their pension income. They both receive pensions of 65 and 72 thousand a year, so can afford it. None of the 4 has a record on the police national computer."

"Thanks Nick. Please do their background checks and flag up their names so I'm informed of any new developments. I'd particularly like to know if one of them dies in suspicious circumstances, especially if they're poisoned. Let's now turn to my morning trip out. I went to Greenford where the maker of this medicine valsartan has their factory. I watched as thousands of capsules were made and packaged into large jars. I saw how those jars were sealed and stored prior to being shipped out to pharmacies. In short, there's no way that a rogue employee could contaminate a single capsule rather than a whole batch. If they did contaminate a whole batch, the quality control that takes a sample from each batch would catch them out. Furthermore, if they did contaminate a batch, there's no way of predicting where it would be sent. Sealed jars are stored, numbered and then dispatched sequentially when an order is received. They go all over the country and no-one could predict which jar would go to which pharmacy. In short, if a capsule was contaminated to form a sealed source of ricin, it must have been done in the Harley Street pharmacy or in Sir John's own house."

"What do you want us to do next, sir?"

"Get those background checks done and meet up here tomorrow at 10 o'clock, because I'm seeing his solicitor first thing Monday morning followed by, *she who must be obeyed.* As it stands, we've no suspect, no-one with means of accessing this poison, several with opportunity to administer it, but none with a motive for doing so. We don't definitely know it was murder, although suicide seems unlikely. It's a real mystery at present, so I need to put my thinking cap on. As it happens, I've got an informal dinner this evening with a few key people who might give us a few insights into this case.

* * *

Painter looked up at the sign above the door and was pleased to see the gesture towards Indian heritage represented by the font; it promised an authentic curry experience transported all the way from the Balti houses of Birmingham. He was delighted that Veronica, his notoriously tight-fisted Superintendent, had agreed to pay for the food, but not surprised she insisted that no costs for alcohol would be reimbursed. He braced himself for a discussion with the professors that would likely be insightful but tending towards him being lectured and peppered with unpronounceable words.

He entered the restaurant and took his place at the end of the table as was appropriate for the host. After ordering an Indian pale ale for himself he had to send the waiter shuttling for more as his guests arrived one by one. Professor Hugh McDermott was first and greeted Painter like a long-lost friend. Soon after, Trisha Green, the Professor of Public Health, originally introduced to Painter by Hugh, arrived and embraced her colleague. This seemed only natural, because they must have known each other for a long time, but Painter was surprised to see that Ruth repeated the process when she arrived. Was this because she had seen the end of Trisha's greeting, or would it have occurred anyway? Hugh and Ruth had been sparring partners during the last case, but the clinch might represent body language denoting mutual admiration and acceptance of their respective positions.

He had expected to start the proceedings by thanking them for all their help with the previous case but was thwarted by the conversation starting with the subject de jour.

"Come on Hugh, tell us what's going to happen next with Covid-19."

"Och, you all know what's going to happen; history

will repeat itself. We've come to the end of the quiet summer period and can be sure that politicians will express surprise when they see the virus reappear as the autumn moves towards winter. The fact that it's a respiratory virus and that these always become prominent every winter will come as entirely novel information to them. The country has, belatedly, learned how to detect the virus now that Boris' chums have been on a learning curve discovering how to run PCR tests, as well as making a mint of money for themselves, so we can already see infections increasing. By next month there will be cases of disease, the hospital wards will be full, intensive care will fill up and the politicians will panic in December. The time to take action is now, but they'll say they need to wait for more evidence. With an exponential process, by the time you have clear evidence it's too late; the cat's already out of the bag."

"Do you think the next wave will affect Christmas?"

"Aye, I'm assuming so and have advised my wife to buy a turkey as usual but leave it in the freezer so our family can celebrate at Easter instead. I think we'll be in lockdown for Christmas. It won't be too bad for us, because we can work over Zoom, but it'll hit unskilled workers badly, just like it did last time."

"I agree with much of that," said Professor Green, "except that you shouldn't describe it as unskilled work. It's work that doesn't need formal qualifications, but it's still skilled. If you don't believe me, try providing the care needs of an elderly relative."

"Aye, you're right, there; I should have said it's different if you're in a people-facing job on a zero hours contract. Such people would clearly benefit from a better career structure, training, paid leave if they come in contact with the virus and recognition of their experience."

"Don't forget that some of them are first generation immigrants, driven to unpack their suitcases here but who still haven't unpacked psychologically," added Ruth. "What do you two professors think about the effects on students, especially the first years who've only just moved to London?"

"They're having a really tough time," said Trisha Green, "especially now they have to pay for their education, unlike Hugh and I who got it free. The revolution of the 60s gave us egalitarianism. It seemed perfect for bright kids from poorer backgrounds to be given access to higher education. The universities expanded and more poor kids became middle class professionals. But the concept that they deserved their progress because they'd worked hard had a dark side; it implied that the other half who didn't go to university had failed. While Germany developed a society with respect for people who use technical skills to earn a living, Britain looked down on them. We got our comeuppance when those people exerted their political rights to vote for Brexit."

"I agree, said Ruth. We need to use the Covid pandemic as a chance for renewal. We need to talk about the rewards of work in terms of esteem as well as pay. Children will remember for all of their lives the banging of pots and pans we did for the NHS, just like the generation before me talks of ration books and air raid sirens. While we clap for the NHS, we need to remember that those doctors and nurses are supported by lots of other non-professional staff, including cleaners, delivery drivers, shelf stackers in supermarkets, childcare workers and those who care for their elderly relatives. We're now calling these people key workers, but also still categorising them as unskilled. We need to change the way we think about them as well as the way we reward them financially."

"Aye, you're correct there. As this hapless government thinks about remedies for inequality it needs to do more than strive to remove barriers to meritocratic progress through society's ranks. We don't need 50% of children to go to university and I don't want to waste my time teaching them things they'll never need. A billionaire entrepreneur in the USA famously compared university diplomas with the indulgences the church used to sell to absolve people of their sins, implying that students have no option but to pay for our pieces of paper if they want a successful career. I'd rather that some youngsters learned to be plumbers so I could pay them a large sum of money to fix my bathroom leak."

The discussion round the table then moved on to how difficult it was to find tradespeople who were skilled, efficient and honest, before lamenting the demise of the fabled Polish plumber. This inevitably led into a long discussion about Brexit:

"The wealthy had a good 2008 crisis caused by their own sort; it was the poor who had to pay for Osborne's illiterate economic decisions that induced austerity. These examples explain why politics turned toxic; Brexit, Trump, Boris; they're all unfair to working people."

"Brexit is a con trick on the poor. It'll satisfy the hedge funds who want anything-goes capitalism in tax-dodging freeports. It'll create a new gravy train as ministers dole out taxpayers' money to their chums."

"I bet you the chancellor will be mean spirited and block a pay rise for the essential workers that he clapped on Thursdays only months ago. He'll also resort to type by playing for political support from the right wing of the Tory party with their *charity begins at home* refrain when he cuts the UK's contribution to overseas development. I bet he'll also refuse to continue the £20 a week uplift to universal credit past the end of March."

"Covid is also largely a disease of the poor. I've seen maps of New York showing where cases of infection and death occurred as the virus arrived in the spring of 2020. The article also showed other maps that superimposed prevalence of HIV. Remarkably, maps of where citizens have a high chance of being sent to prison also fitted well. It's the same sort of people who get hit every time."

These discussions took them through the starters and main courses. Throughout, the couple in their 50s on the next table had barely said a word to each other, thereby demonstrating to Painter that they had been married for many years and knew what the other was thinking without words having to pass between them. In contrast, the four girls in their early 20s occupying the table opposite had gossiped away animatedly throughout the entire evening, talking over each other and interjecting repeatedly, in the way that only the chattering gender could do. The evening was coming to its natural end as the waiters were clearing away before Painter managed to gain the initiative:

"I'm grateful to you all for coming this evening and I'd like to thank you on behalf of the Met for the outstanding advice you gave me in that last case. I hope this meal can act as a small token of our appreciation."

This led to general warm sentiments all round with one reply allowing Painter to pounce:

"Och, you're welcome, Bill. It was great fun so do let me know if you have any others with underlying medical mysteries."

"It's funny you should say that Hugh; I've had a case only this week that's completely flummoxed me."

Painter lent forward to whisper a summary of the case

and the other three moved as well to form a conspiratorial huddle.

"I can give you some background on ricin," said Hugh. "It's a classical case study in undergraduate biochemistry. Many plants contain toxic chemicals to dissuade animals from eating them. Several are related to ricin, but only it has two protein chains that must both be present in order to be toxic; all other plants manage with one. It's a hydrophilic lectin."

"You were doing so well until you lost me with that last part."

"Have you not heard of the yin and yang terms hydrophobic and hydrophilic? The ending *philic* is the opposite of *phobic*. Philic just means that the toxin's soluble in water."

"How do they make caster oil from the beans if they also contain this toxin?"

"Easy. The oil is hydrophobic. Crush the beans, let the oil rise to the top, skim it off and throw away the remaining water."

"Could someone take that water and use it to make ricin at home, in a standard kitchen?"

"Aye, if they knew what they were doing, they could. An undergraduate degree in biochemistry would help though, because you'll lose toxicity if you apply so much heat that the two protein components separate."

"How would you do that in a kitchen?"

Professor McDermott leaned across and whispered in Painter's ear.

"As easy as that?" asked Painter.

"Aye," replied Hugh; "although I'm wondering how they'd monitor for biological activity. They could hardly swallow some to test it out. Your villains may have given doses to animals; mice would be a canny choice. Alternatively, they could look for the large size of protein that represents the two proteins in combination."

"Does that need a sophisticated lab?"

"No, I'd just use thin layer chromatography."

"He means blotting paper," said Professor Green. "Just add the liquid at one end, draw clean water through the blotting paper and add a protein stain. If you boil a sample beforehand, the two chains will separate and run faster on the blotting paper."

"That's actually a good undergraduate practical experiment, although I suspect I'd have difficulty getting it past the health and safety rep."

"Am I right in thinking that a kitchen used for this purpose would be heavily contaminated with ricin?"

"Correct. You'll be able to find it easily for months and months later if you know which kitchen to swab."

Monday 5 October 2020

Painter's morning started with Sir John's solicitor.

"I'm a bit surprised that the decisions set out in his will mean that his estate will pay lots of inheritance tax. I expected a billionaire businessman to save tax wherever possible. Do you have any insight into this?"

"In my experience, Inspector, many young businessmen are motivated in the way you describe. Full of vim and vigour, they bound out into the world of commerce demolishing all before them. Yet, once they've made a billion or two and bought every conceivable luxury several times over, they start to take stock of their lives. They're older now and starting to think of their legacy. They may wish to become benefactors, putting something back into society. If they have offspring, they may wish to establish a dynasty. As you know, Sir John didn't have any children. He became interested in his wife's charity supporting opera, but then found his mark with a charity for veterans who suffered life changing injuries while defending our country. His will allows his wife to be supported in luxury for the rest of her life. The remaining funds will then support the charity for injured servicemen. It's true that about a third will be paid in inheritance tax, but he saw it as his duty to help repay the national debt."

"Did he not seek any publicity for this generous outlook on life?"

"Definitely not. He wished to be someone who helped out behind the scenes."

* * *

Back in New Scotland Yard, Painter got his thoughts in order ready for his next meeting. He'd obtained an appointment because he knew that she liked to be kept informed. As he climbed the stairs, he rehearsed what he was going to say.

The PA asked him to take a seat then, 3 minutes later, told him he could go in. He saw the degree certificate at face level on the wall placed there strategically, he was sure, to intimidate officers like him who hadn't been to university. He turned right and saw the familiar image of Veronica, with severely cropped hair, sitting behind her desk.

"Come in Bill, have a seat and tell me how I can help."

"Well, ma'am; I've come to brief you on a new case that's rather mysterious. It's a VIP whose been poisoned with ricin but we've nobody with means or motive. We've several with potential opportunity, but no strong evidence that any of them did it."

After listening to the whole story and asking a few questions, Veronica gave her opinion:

"If it's not his family members then my guess would be a Russian hitman. We've loads of potential unexplained wealth orders in the pipeline, most of which involve Russians. They've come here under a new government scheme of entrepreneur visas; basically, allowing rich people to buy citizenship. Mark my words and look out for a Russian connection."

* * *

Painter briefed his junior officers on his insights from the dinner last night and from the morning meeting with the solicitor. In return, he heard that the background checks on both the pharmacist and the waitress were clean. Pippa then spoke up:

"As you requested, sir, Nick and I noted on their webpage all the companies owned by Raffles Private Equity and divided them up between us. We searched the national press, local press and social media. All the details are in the file, but we thought you might be interested in one company. It's a story of two lovers of real ale from Liverpool who wanted to start a microbrewery. No bank would lend them money upfront, so they resorted to crowdfunding. They ran a great campaign and raised enough to buy some cheap land in Llandudno, North Wales. A bank then gave them a loan to buy the equipment they needed. Their website goes on about the clean

Snowdon water they use and the fact that they don't filter the product or pasteurize it. It seems that these are important considerations for people who worship real ale. My reading about this taught me that worship is the right word to use. Enthusiasts like beer that's strong on the flavour of hops and thick with resin. It's typically brewed in small batches by independent brewers with followers who buy into the concept of supporting plucky small people to take on the corporate types. So, it's a movement as much as a business. It turns out that making the beer is the easy part; getting it sold is difficult. Microbreweries that are successful often have their own tap room, perhaps just a bar with a couple of tables reached through a door in their industrial base, but it gives a smell of the place and recruits evangelists for the cause."

"Thanks for that insight; how did these two budding entrepreneurs get on?"

"They made an Indian Pale Ale to begin with and started to make sales that would repay some of the bank loan slowly. They also worked on a dark beer, called porter, which was well received by experts but didn't sell well. The net result was that the bank lost patience and stepped in saying they'd broken the strict limits of their financial covenants. The bank said these guys needed extra capital quickly and suggested Raffles Private Equity."

"How did that go down with these lads from Liverpool?"

"Initially, they were pleased to have a saviour; they signed the documents the bank put in front of them and promptly returned to their main interest of brewing beer. The local papers also celebrated the rescue of a local business and the saving of the jobs of the small number of employees. However, 3 months later, these two guys were suddenly removed from the board of the company and given jobs as so-called brand advisors. It was clear from the stories in the press and on social media that the manager of the brewery was now in charge and that his focus was on breaking even financially."

"How was that seen in the press?"

"The local papers accepted the change because of the need to preserve jobs, but social media talked of betrayal of the founders who'd had the vision to set up the company in the first place. Anyway, fast forward four more years and the company was sold to a major brewer. The explanation given was that this would allow the marketing and distribution of the novel beers to accelerate, but social media cried foul. People who'd originally contributed to crowdfunding called it a sell out and said they'd wanted to support an innovative small company doing its own thing, not a major multinational. Some of the comments made on social media are offensive and threatening, including some made by the two founders from Liverpool."

"It's a good lead that's definitely worth looking into,

so get background and financial checks on these Liverpudlians."

Painter was just about to summarise their investigations so far when a ringing tone forced him to look at the iPhone screen:

Frederick Butterworth

"Hello again, Bill. I asked to be put through to you because we've a new case that sounds similar to the last one I gave you. Did you ever get to the bottom of Sir John Pilkington's death?"

"The autopsy showed he died from poisoning but, so far, we've not been able to find a suspect."

"Well, good luck with finding who did it. I'll text you all the details of this new one but be careful because it's another VIP."

Painter read the details then briefed his two junior officers before they set off on the tube to St Paul's. They walked briefly until Painter could stand and admire the Henry VIII gate.

"This recognises the royal connection with the Tudors, although the hospital was founded centuries before; in 1123 if I remember correctly from some recent discussions about plans to celebrate its 900th anniversary."

They located the doctor and listened to the clearly laid out history.

"The patient is Lord Yeast. I gather he's the Chairman of a major brewing company. He was taken ill during a dinner at Brewers' Hall last night and brought here by ambulance. On arrival, his blood pressure was low and he had obvious blood-stained vomitus and faeces. We resuscitated him with fluids, but he'd experienced major damage to his kidneys and liver. We used vasopressor drugs to try to keep his blood pressure up but, despite our best efforts, he expired at 4 AM today. I suspected some form of poisoning so sent forensically labelled samples to Birmingham. I then telephoned the coroner's officer for advice and here you are."

"Thank you doctor for that admirably succinct summary. Please ask the toxicologist to telephone me as soon as he has the results."

As they strode off to their next appointment, Painter had just a few seconds to draw the attention of his colleagues to the beautifully laid out square, surrounded by the classical four wings designed by James Gibbs in the 18th century, at the heart of St Bartholomew's Hospital.

Soon, they were deep in the Barbican at Aldermanbury Square and Painter could announce:

"This building is also remarkable, although it's modern and has a different function. This is Brewers' Hall, the meeting place of the Worshipful Company of Brewers. Before we proceed, is the company headed by Lord Yeast the same one that bought the microbrewery in North Wales that you mentioned?"

"No, sir; it's different."

"That's a shame; it would have linked up our two cases."

They located Lord Yeast's PA. She was a brunette called Carol and was wearing large, tortoiseshell glasses that dominated her appearance. She looked to be in her early thirties and perhaps weighed a little more than she intended. Painter could see that her eyes glistened behind the lenses of the spectacles as she moved her head. They all listened quietly as the still tearful girl told her story.

"Lord Yeast came here at 3 PM for a committee meeting before the dinner arranged for 6:30. As people arrived, I helped them to coffee and then they all took their places around the committee table. After the routine items of apologies for absence and minutes of the last meeting, the first substantive item was to inspect and taste the canapés and fruit beers which we proposed to serve at a future lunchtime meeting."

"Who prepared these items?"

"They were brought in by an external caterer who we've used many times before. She placed a large platter of items onto the side table over there and plated out one of each of the 4 different types of canapé. She placed them in front of each committee member who then tasted them. They then tasted each of 3 fruit beers that had been brewed by us but also served by the caterer. The committee voted, there was a clear preference for two canapés and one fruit beer, so Lord Yeast announced that they were the winners. The caterer removed the plates but left them beside the platters on the side table before retiring to let us continue with our meeting."

"Thank you, Miss, for that clear description on what I know must be a difficult day for you. Now think carefully; could a plate or a glass of beer containing poison have been targeted specifically at Lord Yeast? Was his different in any way or handled differently from the others?"

Carol was pensive for a moment before replying:

"No, I don't think so. The caterer had, I think, 3 small plates in her left hand and two in her right. She placed one of the right-hand plates in front of Lord Yeast and then me, sitting next to him, before using her now free right hand to deliver each of the three plates in her left hand to the next 3 people. She then returned to the side table to collect a further set of 5 plates so that everyone had the same canapés. She then took two beer glasses in her left hand and one in her right to each place around the table. It all happened very quickly, perhaps taking just two minutes to serve us all. Why are you asking; do you think he was poisoned?"

"Thank you for describing that in remarkable detail; do you always have such good recall of events?"

"I have OCD, Inspector. It gives me some problems but does mean I can remember things in great detail."

"Well, I wish all my witnesses were as accurate. I can tell you that we're considering poisoning as a possible cause of death. From what you've said it would have been possible for someone to poison one canapé or one glass."

"But how would someone know which glass or plate was going to be given to Lord Yeast?"

"I don't know, Miss, but it's something we have to follow up. What happened to the plates and glasses?"

"The caterer came back after the committee meeting had ended and took them all away."

"Can I have her name and address please?"

"Of course," said the PA, scrolling through her phone.

"Thank you. Detective Constable Winters will go there now to see if any food and drink remains for forensic examination. Now, think carefully; was there anything out of the ordinary about the committee meeting?"

Carol paused before replying that everything was normal and as expected, so Painter asked her what happened after the committee meeting.

"Committee members chatted for a while, then we went downstairs to prepare for the reception and dinner. Lord Yeast and other members of the procession party needed to put on their regalia. We then went to the reception where champagne was served."

"Was that provided by the same caterer?"

"No, it's our house champagne with our own label. It's stored in our cellar."

"Was a glass brought specially to Lord Yeast?"

Carol paused before replying.

"No, we all walked into the reception room where a member of staff was waiting, holding a silver tray with about 10 glasses of sparkling champagne already poured out. Lord Yeast reached forward to select a glass then made his way into the room. Others did the same and soon we had 75 people chatting away."

"Were the glasses refreshed at any time?"

"Yes, several waiters circulated and topped up glasses as necessary."

"Now think carefully again. Did you see Lord Yeast's glass topped up?"

"Yes, I did, because I was standing next to him throughout the whole afternoon and evening; except, of course, when he went to put on his regalia. Lord Yeast's glass was topped up only once, because he declined a second time, saying he had to keep a clear head before introducing the evening's speaker."

"Did anyone else receive champagne from the bottle that was used to give Lord Yeast a top up?"

"Yes, the waiter came past and filled up about 4 glasses in our group, one after the other."

"Has anyone else from the committee meeting or dinner been taken ill?"

"Not as far as I know, but I'll phone round to them all to check."

"Thank you. What happened next?"

"The Beadle indicated that the procession party should form up. They did this in the corridor while the Beadle announced to the guests that dinner was served. Everyone except those in the procession party made their way through to take their seats according to the seating plan. The Beadle then led the procession party into the banqueting hall to the accompaniment of applause from all of the guests. The procession party took their seats, then starters of smoked salmon were served, beginning with Lord Yeast and the guests."

"Was Lord Yeast's starter plated out and carried straight to him?"

"Yes, it was. Each waiter had 3 plates, two in the left hand and one in the right. It was the plate in the right hand that was given to Lord Yeast."

"That's very precise of you, Miss; I'm pleased that you could see this while you were dealing with your own meal."

"Oh, I wasn't one of the diners, Inspector. I was there standing in the background with the Beadle just in case our services were needed."

"What happened next?"

"The main course of roast beef was served. Again, it was plated and delivered to Lord Yeast first. The dessert of peach melba was then served, again with Lord Yeast served first. After that, the plates were all cleared away. Normally, we would then proceed to the loyal toast followed by a comfort break before Lord Yeast would introduce the speaker. However, Lord Yeast barely touched his peach melba and, remarkably, got up from his chair and left the room."

"Why was that so unusual?"

"No-one ever leaves a dinner before the loyal toast, Inspector. I knew something serious must have happened. The Beadle and I went after Lord Yeast and the Beadle found him in the gentlemen's lavatory. The Beadle came out, told me to call an ambulance and went back in to stay with Lord Yeast. I waited until the paramedics took him away before going back to the banqueting hall where the speeches were coming to an end. I later discovered that the Warden had apologised that Lord Yeast had been called away and gave the introduction to our speaker. Everyone was very surprised to see this deviation from convention which prepared them for the news this morning that Lord Yeast had died."

With that, the girl pulled off her glasses and burst into tears that splashed all over the large lenses. Painter followed his well-worn routine of offering the pristine white linen handkerchief that he kept for this very purpose in his suit pocket.

Painter turned away from the distressed girl to go and

find the Beadle. He confirmed Carol's story, so Painter and Pippa next set off to walk to St Paul's tube station.

"Phone Nick and find out how he's getting on at the caterers. Also, check that it's not the same company who supplied the food for Sir John's fateful lunch; we'd look a bit silly if we missed the fact that our two mysterious cases could be explained by a single cook going on a murder spree."

Before they reached the station, Painter had learned that the caterer was different from the one who supplied the first case. Importantly, she still had the remains of the food and drink from yesterday and Nick was arranging for forensic tests to be done.

"That's great news; tell him to go straight to Totteridge and we'll meet him at the tube station."

The Northern line behaved itself perfectly. The three officers met up and, after a 10-minute walk, could look at a large, detached house with extensive front garden. They walked down a long, winding path to find the door answered by someone called James who introduced himself, remarkably, as the butler.

"Lady Yeast is expecting you, sir," he said as he led them to a large drawing room.

A housekeeper brought in coffee just as Lady Yeast appeared. Painter introduced his team who were invited to sit in comfortable armchairs and a settee all decorated in the same floral pattern. He noted a large antique writing table in the corner with desk telephone, pad of paper and holder for pens. He could not see the finer details of the framed photographs but got the impression that the family included two children.

"Please accept our condolences, Lady Yeast."

"Thank you. I suppose you want to start your questions with the name; most people do. My husband's grandfather was ennobled and thought it would be amusing to acknowledge that brewers' yeast was the source of the family fortune. We've been stuck with it ever since."

"I'm sorry to have to intrude on you at this difficult time, but we suspect your husband might have been poisoned. Can you think of anyone who might want to do that?"

"Of course not; the idea is ridiculous."

"Could you tell us what he ate or drank from the time he woke up yesterday morning?"

"We had a cooked breakfast like we always do. Poached eggs, bacon, sausage and toast. Accompanied by Earl Grey tea without milk. This was all prepared, as usual, by Mrs Jenkins who can give you more details."

"Thank you. Did you eat exactly the same food as your husband did?"

"Yes, Inspector."

"Can I then ask about how your husband travelled to Brewers' Hall?"

"We used to have a chauffeur but once my husband

stepped down to become chairman on a part time basis, we let the man go and now use a local limousine service. They take him to Brewers' Hall or the other place 3 or 4 times a month. James will give you their details while he shows you how to find the other staff."

With that, Lady Yeast rose from her armchair and the 3 officers took the hint to automatically do the same.

"This way, sir;" said James. "Let me give you a guided tour while we locate the others."

The housekeeper was in the kitchen. She told them that all the food came from Waitrose. Nothing remained of the breakfast consumed yesterday except unused tea leaves and the bread that was used to make the toast.

James then took them on a guided tour as if he were an estate agent.

"This house is set within 2 acres of beautifully landscaped gardens, mostly at the rear of the property. The ground floor has a kitchen/breakfast room leading into a dining room. The main reception room leads through a sliding door into a conservatory and then into the garden. There is a cinema room, a games room, a television room as well as utility room, WC and en-suite staff bedroom that is allocated to me. Up on the first floor we have four en-suite bedrooms. The principal bedroom has a vaulted ceiling and terrace overlooking the gardens. A spiral staircase leads to an additional staff en-suite bedroom on the top floor of the house which Mrs Jenkins uses. If you now follow me down to the south-facing gardens, you will see we have many secluded areas. A large terrace runs along the entire width of the house creating an excellent entertaining space. We have a heated outdoor pool and tennis courts over there. The lawn area is beautifully maintained with many mature trees and shrubs. Ah, here is the gardener; Inspector Painter, please let me introduce you to Clive."

The gardener looked to be older than his stated 60 years.

"Do you do all of the work in this large garden?"

"Yes, sir, I do."

"Well, it looks very well kept," said Painter, followed by: "do you have any of these plants?" pointing to the image on Pippa's phone as he did so.

"Oh yes, sir; they're over here."

"Does anyone ever collect the seeds?"

"No, sir; they're poisonous, you see."

"Isn't that a problem having poisonous plants so near to the house?"

"No sir, you can find these in many gardens around the country."

Painter thanked Clive, explained to James that a forensics team would appear soon and was escorted off the premises through the winding pathway.

On the walk back to Totteridge station Painter told them to do financial and background checks on James,

Mrs Jenkins, Clive, the driver of the limousine and the caterer at Brewers' Hall. Pippa then asked:

"What was all that about *the other place* that Lady Yeast mentioned?"

"It's what they call the House of Lords," replied Painter. "I bet Lord Yeast was well known there; the term *beerage* is used to describe those whose families made their fortunes from alcohol. If anyone has any doubt that these people live lives way above the dreams of the rest of us, the little people, then go back for another guided tour from James."

"I'm glad she told us where the name came from," said Pippa; "Lady Yeast sounds to me like a chronic case of thrush."

When they got off the tube train Painter summarised:

"The forensic results on the samples saved by the caterer should be with us by tomorrow afternoon, so meet in my office at 1300 to share what else you've found out in the meantime. Mind you, I've a feeling that all the tests will turn out to be negative, just like with the first case. The only encouraging point is that at least we've got a prime suspect this time."

Pippa and Nick looked at each other before Painter let them into his little joke:

"Don't you read detective stories? It's obvious that the butler did it."

Tuesday 6 October 2020

"Right, let's get started. I spent the morning with the Yeast family solicitor. There's nothing unusual about the will. Everything goes to Lady Yeast until she dies when the estate is divided into two equal parts for their two children. The solicitor thought the Yeasts were happily married and neither of them had consulted her about the possibility of divorce. What have you found out, Nick?"

"I've got the financial check on Mandy Mitchell, sir, the caterer. She owns the company and has had to take on loans to keep it afloat during the pandemic, so is short of cash. However, there's nothing unusual in her company or personal accounts; specifically, no recent payment of an unexplained large sum of money. I also identified the waiters who served Lord Yeast champagne and then food during the dinner and both have clean sheets as well. The same applies to Eric Evans, the driver who took Lord Yeast to Brewers' Hall. I specifically asked if Lord Yeast ate or drank anything during the journey and the driver said no. Like with the first case, the car has been valeted, but I asked forensics to check it out anyway."

"Thanks, Nick. What about you, Pippa?"

"The financial check on Mrs Jenkins is clean, sir. The same goes for James the butler and Clive the gardener, although Clive is often overdrawn at the end of the month."

"In summary then, there's nothing suspicious so far. Let's go through, in chronological order, the opportunities people had to poison him and consider each in turn as we update the whiteboard. Starting with breakfast, Mrs Jenkins would have opportunity to poison his food, while avoiding the wife's. Although the couple both ate the same things, Mrs Jenkins might have slipped something onto his plate. However, we've no motive for such an action. The wife could likewise have done it but has no motive. The ever-present butler potentially had access by providing a drink that he didn't mention to us, but he has no motive. Clive the gardener didn't have access but did have the means, because he showed us the castor oil plants in the flowerbed and he knows they're poisonous. But what would be his motive and how would he deliver the poison? The driver of the limousine had access to Lord Yeast but denies that the man took anything by mouth. Also, he's no motive. Moving on to Brewers' Hall, the PA, Carol, was close to Lord Yeast and seemed distressed at his death. I believe her and think she's an unlikely villain, although she might have had opportunity. The caterer Mandy had opportunity as she handed out plates but has no motive. I think the champagne at the reception is an unlikely vehicle, because the PA told us there was a tray of drinks and Lord Yeast could have selected any one of them. We know that only one glass could have been poisoned because no-one else has been taken ill. We need to pause at this point, because someone wishing to kill any one of the attending people at random could have used the champagne glass method. But what would be the motive? Also, now that we have two cases of poisoned rich men it does look as if Lord Yeast was targeted. No, overall, I think the champagne is very unlikely. The same goes for the champagne top up because the same bottle was used to give drinks to several people. We now move on to the dinner. The starter was plated out, so the waiter, but not the chef, could have targeted the food to the victim. The same goes for the main course, but what was the motive? I'm discounting the dessert because Lord Yeast was already feeling ill by the time it arrived. There, I think that's the chronology; have I left anything out?"

"No, sir; but it's all very mysterious, so what should we do next?"

"We need to wait to see if forensics gives us a location for the crime."

As if on cue, Painter's phone rang and he jotted notes while listening to the person at the other end. He then gave a summary to his two officers:

"All the tests are negative. Not a drop of ricin was found at any site; not in the kitchen or the house, the limousine, the reception room, the caterer's food or her kitchen, or the banqueting room. Yet our victim was full of the stuff, as was the gentleman's loo at Brewers' Hall where he was taken ill. The poison got into him somehow, but we don't know when or how. It's consistent with a closed source of poison that we were told about for the first case. The toxicologist has also tested the valsartan capsules that belonged to Sir John. They came up negative as well so, if a capsule was used to poison him, it was only one in the whole batch."

"Where do we go now, sir?"

"I'm going to follow up on the possibility of an individual drug capsule being the source and will start by interviewing his doctor. Meanwhile, I'll allocate some different avenues of investigation that you can follow up on."

Painter thought about the skills of the two junior officers in front of him. Nick was skilled at basic plodding police fact checking, but what could he do with a recent graduate?

"Let's start with a task for you, Pippa. I wonder if someone's playing a game here following the plot of some famous story, only substituting ricin for the original poison. Draw upon your degree in English literature to give me a brief summary of plotlines that involve poisonings and the motivation behind them. No more than three pages of A4 mind you; I don't have time to read a thesis. We then need to build on the things we definitely do know. It's pretty obvious that our two cases are linked, so let's look for connections between the pair of them. Both victims have something in common; their whereabouts were known. Sir John's staff issued an agenda as did Lord Yeast's for their meetings. Anyone planning to murder them would know exactly where they would be at a pre-ordained time, as long as they'd seen the agendas. So, my question to you both is: who's on the two circulation lists? Also, did our victims have any personal links, like membership of the same golf club, or any business connections? Check also for any connections between each of the individuals we've come across so far. Nick: get their phone records and cross reference to see if any one of them has contacted another. I don't care who they are and have no preconceived ideas, but we're going to find the bastard if it's the last thing I do."

Wednesday 7 October 2020

The large hand of the clock was approaching the upright position, so Painter set off to walk upstairs. On the way, while silently finalising his summary of how the investigation was, or was not, progressing, he wondered why she'd sent for him. He was waved through into the inner sanctum by her PA, glanced at the framed degree certificate and turned right to find that Veronica had a guest.

"Inspector Bill Painter, meet Commander Nigel Rogers from the Counter Terrorism Unit. I've asked him here to listen to your unusual cases of ricin poisoning and consider if his unit should get involved now that we've had two cases. Please give him a brief summary of both of the victims and your investigations so far."

Painter hadn't been prepared for this but knew the cases like the back of his hand. He gave a ten-minute summary and answered several questions from the Commander, before awaiting his conclusion.

"Thank you, Inspector. I can't fault what you've done so far and wish you good luck in trying to solve your mystery. I can't see any obvious links to terrorism and there's been no Internet chatter about poison recently, so I don't think we need to get involved officially at this stage. However, I can offer to second an observer to join your team if that would help."

"Thank you, Nigel; I'm sure Inspector Painter would welcome some assistance."

After that fait accompli Painter could only offer his thanks and enquire about the officer's past experience.

"She's a judge from Afghanistan who's recently been evacuated by the Foreign Office from Kabul. She's quite a tough character, as you might imagine from a woman in that country who's been sentencing members of the Taliban for crimes they've committed. I'll email you her personnel file today and tell her to report to you at 09:00 tomorrow."

While walking down the stairs back to his office, Painter wondered why Veronica had engineered a review of progress by another senior officer. Was she losing confidence in Painter's ability to solve the crimes? Would Nigel Rogers' conclusion: **I can't fault what you've done so far** get her off his back? Should he consider this new woman from Afghanistan to be an assistant for him or a spy within his team, reporting back to Nigel and then Veronica?

* * *

Back home in his study, Painter poured himself a glass of malt whisky, selected a CD by Oscar Peterson and settled down to think through the cases. What could be the objectives of removing two rich industrialists from the face of the earth? Is the first death the reason why the second had to occur? Are there other businesspeople whose lives are next in line? Could he anticipate who they might be and so take action to protect them? Had he missed anything? If there were to be additional cases, could he be held responsible for not preventing them? Would Veronica be down on him like a ton of bricks if there was another case, or would she support him through thick and thin? His mind kept returning to these questions like a bruise that he felt compelled to press to check if it was still tender.

The CD ended so he selected another by the same pianist, refilled his glass and turned to the personnel file on his laptop. As he went through it, he acknowledged how brave she'd been. Baako was born in 1970 and qualified as a lawyer. She fled to Pakistan when the Taliban took over in 1997 and returned to Afghanistan 10 years later. She sat as a judge until, anticipating withdrawal of US troops, she requested asylum in the UK. There was an obvious risk to her life if the Taliban fighters she had sent down were released from prison, so her request was looked upon favourably. The Foreign Office assigned her to the Counter Terrorism Unit.

Painter looked away from the screen to get his thoughts in order. Although she had shown bravery in her own country, what use could she be to him in his? If Veronica was correct and he was dealing with Russian ricin, how could this woman possibly help? In short, would Baako be more of a hindrance than a help, even if she wasn't a spy within his team?

Thursday 8 October 2020

At exactly 9 o'clock, Painter's phone rang to say that a lady was waiting for him in reception. He found a plump woman in her early 50s wearing a loose-fitting dress that obscured any feminine curves plus a thin head-scarf. He took her back to his office and introduced her to Pippa and Nick.

"Why don't you give us a brief summary of your experience so far and suggest how you may be able to help us?"

"Thank you, Inspector Painter. My name is Baako; it means first-born in my language. I was born in Afghanistan and obtained a law degree from Kabul university. When the Taliban took over in 1997, I moved to Pakistan where I kept myself by teaching schoolchildren. I also took a judiciary course part time. After 9-11 I was able to return to my country and worked on the new judicial code. This was a difficult balancing act for a country with traditional Islamic law coupled with new external donors who wanted to see their own values incorporated, including equal rights for women. Eventually, in 2004, the new code was agreed. I then worked as a judge in the family affairs court where I heard cases of murder, rape and forced marriage. I gave guilty verdicts to many Taliban males who threatened me personally, vowing to kill me as soon as they were released from prison. The imminent withdrawal of USA troops brought that day forward, so I applied to the UK for asylum. Here I am and I hope my skills and knowledge will be transferable to your cases."

"Thank you and I must say I admire your bravery. Pippa will now give a summary of our two cases of poisoning and I'd be interested to hear what you think."

As soon as Pippa had finished, Baako gave her opinion without hesitation:

"This could be commercial, driven by business rivalries. It could be personal. It could derive from family conflicts with grudges maintained over generations, as I've seen in Afghanistan many a time. Whether any of those could be termed terrorism depends on the definition given. In states with dominant leaders, anyone who disagrees with the Great Leader must be a terrorist."

"Thank you for that insight, Baako. I'll leave you with Nick and Pippa to show you around. You won't see me again today because I have to go off to another appointment. I'm sure my colleagues will explain to you that tomorrow is a day off for all of our team so you won't need to come in. Enjoy your free time and I'll see you all here at 08:00 on Saturday."

* * *

Painter walked to Embankment station and took the Bakerloo line to Baker Street followed by a walk to his next destination. The address in Harley Street was different than that for the first case but the decor and imperious attitude of the doctor were similar.

"I really cannot tell you very much, Inspector. Lord Yeast was a longstanding patient of mine with hypertension as his only significant medical condition that was well controlled with valsartan."

Painter's ears pricked up at the mention of the now familiar drug.

"Is this a commonly prescribed drug?"

"Oh yes; it's now one of our preferred treatments for hypertension because it's effective and has few side effects. In the past we used to give diuretics but the inevitable requirement to pass large volumes of urine did not fit in with the lifestyle of my busy patients. If they don't like a drug, they'll stop taking it and no medicine can work if it's left in the bathroom cabinet."

"Do you use a pharmacist here in Harley Street to dispense your prescriptions?"

"Yes, we do, but I'll need to leave you in the careful hands of our receptionist to give you all the details."

After being summarily dismissed, Painter had a feeling of deja vu as he was guided down to the basement and along a tunnel that led into a dispensary which was different to the one he'd seen before but where he saw capsules and tablets being dispensed in the same traditional way. He left with contact details for the junior pharmacist who had processed Lord Yeast's last prescription as well as a printout of 5 other patients who were receiving the drug.

* * *

After a quick journey on the District line to Mile End and the number 277 bus to Hackney, Painter wolfed down the supper that Betty had prepared for him before settling down in his study to do some thinking. He poured a glass of whisky and selected a CD by Thelonious Monk before turning to Pippa's paper. It was typewritten but had a handwritten covering note which allowed him to discover her attractive discursive style, with large loops decorating many letters to give a flowery appearance, akin to a sign you might see outside a bric a brac store. Painter wasn't sure why he was surprised by this, before considering that he rarely saw people's handwriting any more as they communicated with emails or texts.

Hello sir; here are the summaries of the 10 poisonings that I told you about from the Guardian, written by John Mullen. I've put them in chronological order for you, from 8 AD to 1999. The summaries are very brief as you asked but I'd be happy to provide more details if you need them.

Pippa

8AD Metamorphoses by Ovid

There are 15 books in total. In the ninth, Hercules discovers a centaur called Nessus raping his wife, Deianira. Hercules shoots him with an arrow dipped in the poisonous blood of the Hydra. As he dies, Nessus tells Deianira that centaur blood acts as a love potion so she soaks a robe in it and gives it to Hercules. However, it's poisonous and wracks her husband with such pain that he begs for death.

1589 The Jew of Malta by Christopher Marlowe

Barabas poisons his own daughter Abigail because she's become a Christian and joined a nunnery, but he has to kill all the other nuns as well in the order to get to her.

1600 Hamlet by William Shakespeare

Hamlet seeks revenge against his uncle, Claudius who has murdered Hamlet's father in order to seize his throne and marry Hamlet's mother. Poison accounts for four of the play's leading characters. During a fencing match, Hamlet and Laertes are both poisoned by the same contaminated rapier. Gertrude quaffs the poisoned drink intended by Claudius for her son. Claudius then gets a poisoned stab from Hamlet, who also makes him drink the potion.

1606 The Revenger's Tragedy by Christopher Middleton

This Jacobean tragedy features an ingenious example of poisoning. Vindice revenges the poisoning of his beloved Gloriana when she rejected the advances of the lustful Duke: the lecherous ruler is conned into kissing Gloriana's skull, to which poison has been applied.

1845 The Laboratory by Robert Browning

This consists of a monologue spoken by a resentful, spurned lover, looking for revenge. He takes poison to a dance and gives her a contaminated present.

1890 The Sign of Four by Arthur Conan Doyle

This was Conan Doyle's second novel featuring Sherlock Holmes. It involves double crossing over stolen treasure. When Sherlock investigates the locked room murder of Bartholomew Sholto, he identifies what appears to be a poisoned thorn lodged in the victim's skin. His anthropological knowledge tells him that the killer was an Andaman Islander who had used a poisoned dart.

1934 I, Claudius by Robert Graves

In this fictional memoir of the Roman emperor the most

prolific poisoner is Livia, the narrator's grandmother and wife of the emperor Augustus. Augustus, scared of being poisoned, eats only figs he picks for himself from a tree, but he dies mysteriously anyway; the poison was painted onto the fruit hanging on the branch.

1936 Cards on the Table by Agatha Christie

The husband of one of Dr Roberts' patients dies of anthrax shortly after accusing the doctor of improper conduct. Hercule Poirot reveals that Dr Roberts painted *Bacillus anthracis* onto the victim's shaving brush which killed him once a nick from his razor provided access to his blood.

1971 A Shroud for a Nightingale by PD James

Trainee nurse Jo Fallon dies in a nursing home from insecticide slipped into her whisky. In finding the culprit, Inspector Dalgleish uncovers lesbian passions and a matron with a Nazi past.

1999 A Series of Unfortunate Events by Lemony Snicket

The Reptile Room is the second of 13 novels in this Gothic book aimed at children. Uncle Monty, a keen keeper of snakes, is found dead, apparently following a bite from one of his own animals. In reality, this benevolent guardian of orphans has been poisoned by the fiendish Count Olaf, who is after the money that supports the institution.

The CD had moved on to the jazz pianist's interpretation of *smoke gets in your eyes* which Painter thought summarised nicely his lack of clear vision about these cases. He refreshed his glass of whisky, took out a pad of lined paper and made even briefer summaries of the information provided by Pippa:

Sex
Religion
Sex, ambition, family
Sex
Sex
Money
Sex, power, family
Sex
Sex, hidden secret
Money

It seemed that the author of the Guardian article had pointed him towards sex, money and family as being the most common forces that the reading public had accepted over millennia as valid justifications for poisoning. Which of these, if any, were at the heart of his current cases? He'd seen no suggestion of a sexual motive so far. Baako had suggested a family connection but there was no evidence of any link between any of the people involved. Painter always said that money's behind many a mischief so selected this as his most likely explanation for the crimes, inflicted as they were on rich people. He decided what tasks he would give his junior staff and retired for the night, pleased with his evening's work.

Friday 9 October 2020

Painter enjoyed the luxury of a lie-in while listening to Radio 4. He eventually got up when he could resist no more the aroma of the cooked breakfast Betty was preparing in the kitchen. He devoured the meal known as the full English, using freshly brewed tea to wash down the tablet he had to take daily for his hypertension; valsartan, exactly the same drug as taken by the first victim, Sir John and the second, Lord Yeast. He was just getting into the shower when his phone rang to declare that his day was about to change.

Frederick Butterworth

"You won't believe it Bill, but I've got another case for you that sounds similar to the other two. Did you ever get to the bottom of what happened to them?"

"No, Fred; inquiries are still progressing but no answer so far."

"Well, this one might give you a clue to help with the others. I'll text all the details but, from my point of view, it's a doctor who can't issue a death certificate and suspects poisoning. Oh, and it's a VIP, just like the other two."

Painter punched the red button on his iPhone, rushed through his ablutions and called to Betty:

"Sorry love, I've got to go to work."

"But we were going to look at sofas together; you promised."

"I know and I apologise, but you know how it is in my business; murder trumps upholstery."

The journey on the 277 gave him time to phone Nick and Pippa and ruin their days off as well. He decided to ask them not to contact Baako; his excuse was that she could do with the time off, but the real reason was he didn't yet know if he could trust her. The other person he'd mislead was his wife; in truth, he would much rather be hunting villains that shopping for sofas but wouldn't say that to Betty. At Mile End he caught a Hammersmith and City tube train straight to Paddington.

Painter met up with his two junior officers and guided them round to the now familiar façade of a recently built NHS hospital. He met the doctor in the intensive care unit on the ninth floor, listened to the history, checked that samples had been taken for toxicology and set off to visit the family home where the victim had been taken ill.

For the benefit of Pippa, who had only recently arrived in London, he explained that they would take the Circle line to Kings Cross then change onto the Northern line to Archway, making sure to choose the correct branch going North. After leaving the station they walked for 5-10 minutes to reach their destination; a detached house in a fashionable area. Painter showed his warrant card to the elderly, stooped woman who answered the door wearing a floral apron with bulging front pockets. She turned out to be the cleaning lady and assumed she was obliged to tell Painter everything she knew, starting with her name; Mrs Williams.

"Mrs Randall's terribly upset, as you can imagine. He was taken ill here last night after supper. She dialled 999 and the ambulance came quickly but they couldn't do much to help him. It's all come as such a shock, you see. Shame really, because they made a nice couple, very happy here. Of course, they're rattling round in this four bedroomed house now that Robert and Roberta have left home."

"Is this the children in the photograph on the side-board?" asked Painter, as a way of shutting the woman up.

"Yes, dear; that's them."

As he looked, the photograph displayed in the silver frame moved sideways to be replaced with another. This was clearly some modern, digital photo frame that Painter hadn't come across before. In quick succession, he saw images of Mr Randall, Mrs Randall, daughter, son and dog before the husband reappeared.

"Thank you for all of this information. Could you now check to see if Mrs Randall feels up to talking to us?"

Painter had a good look round the property while waiting and eventually turned to see a middle-aged woman enter the room. She had silver hair and her glasses dangled from a chain round her neck.

"I'm so sorry to disturb you at this difficult time, Mrs Randall, but if you could answer one or two questions it would help our investigation."

The woman nodded, but looked uncertain what to do next, so Painter guided her to sit in an armchair while he, Pippa and Nick settled into a large sofa, not unlike the one he knew Betty had been keen to look at today.

"Can you start by telling us what you and your husband had for breakfast yesterday?"

Once Mrs Randall started to speak, she gave clear answers to factual questions, although Painter doubted if she was up to speculating on why her husband had been poisoned.

"We both had muesli with almond milk followed by toast and marmalade. We also shared a pot of Earl Grey tea."

"Did your husband then set off for work?"

"Yes, he did. A car collects him every morning. It seems silly to me when he runs London Transport, but it's not easy to get to Stratford from here."

"What time did your husband return home?"

"It was about 6:30. I had a goat cheese salad ready and had made the broth for moules mariniere so just added the mussels once he'd arrived. I served it with hunks of baguette; it was his favourite meal."

With that, floods of tears burst forth. Painter produced the clean, freshly laundered white handkerchief he had ready for such circumstances, but it was several minutes before he felt he could continue his questioning.

"Do you think you could answer just one or two more questions?"

"Yes, I'll try. I'm so sorry Inspector, but we were married for 24 years and this has all come as such a shock."

"I understand that and am grateful to you for helping us. Did you eat the same evening meal as your husband did?"

"Yes, exactly the same and we shared a bottle of *Chenin blanc* as well."

"Where does all of your food come from?"

"It's delivered by M&S."

"At what time was your husband taken ill?"

"At about 9 o'clock he said he felt unwell. He walked about a bit to see if trapped wind in his tummy would pass, but then went to the downstairs loo and was sick. When he tried to stand up, he was as white as a sheet and was unsteady on his feet. I could see blood around his mouth so phoned 999 immediately. They came very quickly and I went with him in the ambulance to St Mary's. He was sick again during the journey. They rushed him into A&E and, after about half an hour, took him to intensive care. I stayed outside the doors waiting, but the doctor came to tell me that William had died at about 3 AM."

With that, the tears flowed again and Painter had to reach for his reserve handkerchief. He knew he would get nothing more from the witness today, so the team made their exit. On the way out, he advised Mrs Williams that a forensic team was on its way to examine the house. They set off for Highgate tube station, with Painter talking while walking:

"That was all very sad. It's the phase of life known as empty nesting. A couple bring up children and are left with a large house once the kids set off to find their own way in the world. It affects people in different ways; some enjoy the free time they now have while others pine away for their lost function in life. I wonder which way it turned out for the Randalls?"

"Do you think it's relevant, sir?

"Anything might be relevant; just note the details for now."

"Are we going to his office now, sir?"

"Yes, Pippa; we are. He may have been in charge of London Transport but doesn't seem to know much about the practicalities of moving about our capital city. We'll go South on the Northern line to Kentish Town, walk for 5-10 minutes to Camden Road and then get the North London line straight to Stratford. It should be an easy and quick journey, so if he didn't tell his wife about it, what else was he hiding from her? Perhaps he's one of those people who like to have their ego flattered by the appearance of a car and driver outside their house every morning."

At Endeavour Square they located the building that housed William Randall's office and asked for his office to be called. Within minutes, Painter discovered another example of an efficient woman supporting her boss as his secretary strode up to the three of them. She was called Louise and was strikingly attractive. Aged about 28 she was tall and trim with a generous bust, blonde hair, high cheekbones and a wide, soft mouth that looked as if it would normally display a welcoming smile. On this occasion however, her obvious beauty was marred by red, swollen eyes and tense facial features suggesting she was trying hard to stop herself from crying any more. Painter regretted that both of his clean handkerchiefs had been used; he'd left one in the hand of the weeping Mrs Randall but had the second one, damp, in his jacket pocket that, he supposed, could be pressed into service in an emergency. His questioning quickly ascertained that William Randall had drunk plenty of black, filter coffee without sugar during the day but had not stopped for anything to eat at lunchtime. In fact, he hadn't eaten anything at all that day, as was his usual practice because of his busy schedule of work. The secretary had prepared three separate pots of coffee for him during the day and had drunk some of it herself. She had also served it to colleagues who joined him for meetings at 10, 11 and again at 3. He had not left his office at lunchtime and so could not have eaten anything purchased outside.

Once they had left the building, Painter told Nick and Pippa to get full background and financial checks, as they had done for the previous cases, on the wife, the cleaning lady the chauffeur and the secretary. He told them to return to get formal statements tomorrow before meeting in his office at 14:00. He also asked Pippa to make an appointment to see the solicitor to review the will. He then told them they could escape for the rest of the day, because they were supposed to be having a day off and there was little more they could do until the toxicology results came through.

Painter set off to return home to Hackney noting, with a smile, that there would not now be time to go shopping. He just hoped that Betty would still speak to him and make him an evening meal.

Saturday 10 October 2020

Painter read the formal interviews of all the people as they came through from Nick and Pippa by email.

His phone rang earlier than expected:

"We're getting better and better at processing ricin tests. You've already sent us more requests than we normally get in 5 years. However, I'm afraid all the results from the sites you sampled are negative again. I've re-run all the samples from the previous cases and they're still completely negative. I've checked the assay and it's working as expected. Also, the clinical samples from your William Randall are strongly positive so I'm convinced I'm giving you true negative results for all the rest. I can only suggest, again, that your victims were poisoned using closed sources."

The junior staff arrived at the chosen hour but were too late to hear the lab results first hand.

"Baako; there was a development yesterday that you missed. In summary, we had a third case that's very similar to the first two. It means we didn't have a rest day after all."

"I would have joined you yesterday if someone had phoned me."

"Thank you Baako; I'll bear that in mind if we get any more cases. Now, listen to the update from Nick and

Pippa. Their witness statements sound similar to those from the first two cases. I suppose the only encouraging slant I can put on this is that we have consistent results from all 3 murders," announced Painter. "What have you both been able to find out?"

"As you requested, sir, we've checked the circulation list for the agendas of the meetings held by Sir John and Lord Yeast. All the people who received them are already on our radar. We've done full background and financial checks on the brewery guys from Liverpool and found nothing suspicious. We then went through all the calls made by each phone number belonging to the people in cases 1 and 2 as provided by British Telecom, Virgin or Vodafone. There's not a single example of any phone from any of our potential suspects speaking to or texting any other suspect."

"That's disappointing, but now you'll need to add the phone numbers from all the people associated with case 3."

"I still think this could be some sort of family feud," volunteered Baako.

"Thanks for the suggestion," sighed Painter, "but do you have any evidence to support any family or other links between any of these people?"

Receiving no answer, Painter continued:

"I'm always keen for officers to follow up any hunches they may have during a case, so go through the CVs of all the people in the 3 cases and see if they're related in any way, Baako and report back to the group on Monday."

Pippa waited until the three junior officers were clear of Painter's office before she announced:

"Now do you see what I mean, Baako? He dismissed your suggestion without putting any resources into checking out the possibility. I'm sure it's because you're a woman; he doesn't want intelligent women to solve the case for him."

"I have experienced much worse in my life so can't complain. Also, I would have come to meet you all yesterday if you had phoned me to say a development had occurred in the cases."

"I know you would have, Baako, but he told us not to disturb you. It's further evidence that he feels he doesn't need women in his team."

"I wasn't surprised that he just assumed we'd come in on our official rest day because that's the way he's always worked, but now Pippa has mentioned it, he does take us all for granted," added Nick.

* * *

Painter poured out a glass of malt whisky, selected Oscar Peterson and let the mellow liquid and mellow music soothe his troubled brain for a few moments. He then read again all the witness statements his staff had obtained and reflected on their performance.

They had done well with the routine police work but none of them had made a suggestion leading to a likely villain. Nick was, as always, very solid in his investigations. Painter's new Sergeant had produced a literary list of possible reasons for administering poison but her degree in English literature had not helped otherwise. The unusual, albeit brave, woman recently arrived from Afghanistan seemed obsessed with the possibility of a family feud. Painter could buy this possibility, were it not for the complete absence of any evidence of two people crossing swords with each other, or even having contact, at any time. He'd have to keep an eye on her to make sure she wasn't trying to lead people down the wrong path. He'd also be careful around her in case she was a plant, reporting back to Nigel and Veronica.

Painter took another sip of the amber nectar and wondered if he was getting a bit paranoid. This had happened before under stress and he knew why he was stressed this time; Veronica showed all the signs of planning to bring in another officer to lead the investigation if he failed. He was as disappointed as she was that he didn't have a suspect in sight, but the cases were very complex and confusing. He also felt guilty that another person might die due to his inability to crack the cases.

The music came to the final track, Painter drained

the glass of the last drop of malt and made a decision. It wasn't paranoia to ask if, overall, these two new women were helping or hindering his investigation. As he quelled the magnificent music machine for the night, he resolved to test the women further by giving them additional tasks once the weekend was over.

Monday 12 October 2020

His usual journey by bus and then tube provided plenty of time for Painter to contemplate how he could combine the training programme that Veronica told him to work on for junior officers with his investigation into multiple murders. He needed to kill two birds with one stone, if that wasn't a mixed metaphor, given the cases he was dealing with. At the 8 AM meeting in his office he started with some background:

"Everything's going so fast with these cases that we need to pause from time to time to take stock of where we are. For the second case, Lord Yeast, I'm adding to the whiteboard the details of a young pharmacist who needs full financial and background checks please. I'm also adding the names of 5 more people who received valsartan from a second dispensary in Harley Street. Still get their names flagged up in case they die from poisoning, but I think this is now a less fruitful line of enquiry. We were thinking that the capsules might have been intended for someone else, but now we have 3 cases who are all male, wealthy VIPs, I suggest we can leave that possibility on the back burner for now. Let's stand back and look at what we've got so far."

Painter paused for emphasis and, receiving no questions, continued:

"We don't have a motive for any of these murders. We have the means, in terms of ricin poison, but don't know how it was administered to any of the three victims, although we know it must have been swallowed. We should therefore focus on opportunity. If we assume these three people did not commit elaborate and coordinated suicides, then at least one person in each case must have administered the poison. Our cases are obviously connected, so we need to look for common features among them. We need to put ourselves in the shoes of those planning these crimes and consider what they would need in order to achieve their aims. For example, they may have an insider on each of three teams. That means that three people we've interviewed so far must know more than they're telling us. They may not have understood that they were delivering a fatal poison, because they may have been misled by the organiser of these crimes, but they have important information that could lead us to this mastermind. They may be feeling scared at the moment, now that they see they've helped to commit murder, but we need to find them and tell them our main target is the person in charge, not the people he's dragged into his net."

"That's a bit like the women who were tricked into giving poison to the brother of the dictator of North Korea," said Pippa. "Have you any idea who our conspirators might be, sir?"

"No, Pippa; not yet. But we can imagine some possibilities. We've been advised that the poison may have been sealed within food. The mastermind would therefore need people who could deliver the poison this way. Who have we seen who could fit the bill?"

"The two caterers."

"Exactly, Pippa. You've done the standard background and financial checks. Now show Baako how we check all social media for connections between the pair of them and report back here at 15:00. If you follow the logic of access to food, then the mastermind may have used people with access to food in this third case. Nick: find out exactly who selected and packed the food at M&S that was sent to the house of William Randall."

* * *

Everyone was on time for the 3 PM meeting and Pippa spoke up first:

"Baako and I have checked all social media for every suspect and listed the names of people tagged in photos. We created a mini database in *Holmes* and cross checked all names but not one of our suspects appears on any site except their own."

"That's a shame; what about you, Nick?"

"I've found out the employee at M&S who packed the food that Mr Randall ate. They keep excellent records just in case a customer complains they've been sent the wrong item. The packer's name is Brian Richards. He's aged 20 and has worked for them since he left school. I located him at work and took a routine statement from him. Apparently the Randalls have a regular order, so he recognised the list of items. He said everything was normal when he selected the items from the shelves, with nothing to indicate that seals had been broken. He denied tampering with any of the packages. He's single and lives with his parents in Muswell Hill, in a house near to the M&S store. I've requested full background and financial checks on him."

"That's good as far as it goes. We now need to consider a different avenue of investigation. Another thing these cases have in common is a succession of young women apparently devoted to their bosses. What if they were just playing that role in order to deceive us? What if they had been recruited by the mastermind for assassination? Even better; what if our imagined mastermind has been planning this for years and trained them and placed them in position well before they were told to activate their plans?"

"You mean like sleepers in spy movies, sir?"

"Yes, exactly like that, Pippa. So, track back through the lives of the three of them. I'd be particularly interested to hear if they all attended the same secretarial school."

Tuesday 13 October 2020

Painter was just settling into his morning routine when his iPhone rang, causing him to groan as he saw the name displayed:

Frederick Butterworth

He tapped the green button to find his worst fears confirmed.

"Bill: there's been another one. The same doctor at St Mary's who looked after the last case has just telephoned me. A patient called Günter Müller was admitted last night as an emergency and died this morning. The doctor can't issue a death certificate and says he suspects poisoning; wait for it, poisoning with ricin. Can you believe it? These cases are getting so common that this doctor can tell us the likely poison. I'll text you all the details, but you won't be surprised to hear that the patient's a VIP. What do you think's going on? Are we going to get any more cases? My desk is bulging with case files on them and the coroner's not happy."

"I share your concerns Fred, but I've no answers for you yet. We'll investigate this case just like we've done with the others and let you know when we've found something concrete. Please tell the coroner that we're working flat out on this."

Painter ended the call and rallied his troops:

"Right, you lot; we're off to Peru again."

Baako looked confused, so Pippa whispered to her as they walked along that Painter was making a rather weak joke about a character in children's books and now films called Paddington Bear (who was born in Peru).

They came out of the tube station and Painter checked his phone for any missed messages. After a brief walk, he could stare up, once again, at the façade of the new St Mary's Hospital. He entered the Queen Elizabeth the Queen Mother building and followed the familiar route to the intensive care department on the ninth floor.

"Hello, Inspector Painter. I didn't expect to see you again so soon but thought it likely once I saw the patient last night. His constellation of symptoms is unlike any natural disease and very similar to those I saw in the unfortunate Mr Randall. There's no doubt in my mind that this new patient also died from poisoning and I suspect ricin as the cause because of what was found during the post mortem of the last case. I've sent samples to Birmingham toxicology having followed the instructions for maintaining chain of custody. Do you think we should be preparing to receive further cases? Should I be training my junior staff in what to look out for?"

"I can't answer those questions yet, doctor. We're following several leads and will let you know as soon as we can."

Painter led his junior officers to the Jubilee line and got off the train at St John's Wood. After a five-minute walk, he showed his warrant card to gain entrance to a modern block and was then let into a large apartment by a middle-aged woman who introduced herself as Mrs Roberts, the cleaning lady. She led the way past painters and decorators working in a bedroom and guided the police officers to sit in comfortable chairs that, like the rest of the furniture, were Scandinavian in design, with simple, square lines and pale grey cushions. In place of curtains, it had grey blinds hanging vertically. This was all a bit too stark for Painter's liking, but he knew it was fashionable.

Eventually, Mrs Müller came into the room, wearing a towelling dressing gown. She wore no makeup and her hair was dishevelled but it was clear that she would cut an attractive figure under normal circumstances. The cleaning lady guided her into a square chair and sat in an adjoining chair, holding her hand.

"I'm very sorry to have to disturb you at this difficult time, Mrs Müller, but could you help us by answering one or two questions?"

The woman nodded, but Painter was not sure how much help she'd be today.

"Let's start with breakfast. What did your husband eat yesterday morning?"

Hannah Müller replied in an obvious German accent:

"We always have plain yoghurt to which we add fresh fruit. Yesterday it was blueberries."

"And after that?"

"We always have Bircher muesli plus black filter coffee."

"Did your husband eat anything else?"

"No, Inspector."

"Did you eat the same food?"

"Yes, Inspector."

"Where does your food come from?"

"It's delivered by the supermarket that Günter works for. Oh, I should say worked, shouldn't I?"

With that, Mrs Müller burst into tears. Painter reached for his trademark freshly washed and ironed white handkerchief, which was soon soggy. After a few minutes the wife regained her composure and Painter asked if he could ask her one or two more questions. Receiving a nod from behind the handkerchief he asked:

"What time did he leave for work and how does he travel there?"

"He leaves; that is, he left, at 8 o'clock exactly. He takes the Jubilee line tube train to Neasden to the new office block of the company."

"What time did he return from work?"

"He arrived at 7 PM in time for supper. I had prepared a veal schnitzel with new potatoes and broccoli."

"Did he eat all of the meal?"

"Yes, Inspector."

"And did you eat the same food?"

"Yes, Inspector."

"I understand that your husband was taken ill last night. Can you tell me when?"

"We had eaten our meal and cleared away the plates. We settled down to watch the television, but he soon said he felt uncomfortable. He had pains in his stomach; like wind, only worse. He went to the bathroom and I heard him being sick. This was so unusual that I was concerned for him. I opened the door and could see blood in the lavatory. I telephoned for an ambulance and asked the concierge to direct them to our apartment urgently. The people, the paramedics, came quickly, put Günter in a wheelchair and took him down in the lift. I went with him in the ambulance, holding his hand, but he didn't really know I was there. They rushed him to the casualty department and then, after about 30 minutes, to intensive care. A doctor came to tell me that Günter was seriously ill, but they were doing all they could. In the early hours of the morning the doctor came back to tell me the terrible news that my husband had died."

The tears that now flowed threatened to overwhelm Painter's already sodden handkerchief, so he took his leave, asking the cleaning lady to stay with Mrs Müller. He said that a forensic team would soon appear and that his officers would return tomorrow to take statements.

Once they were out on the pavement in St John's Wood, Painter spoke to Pippa and Nick:

"This is like a repeat of the other cases. We need to wait for forensics but can assume that someone poisoned Günter Müller with ricin. We'll now go on the Jubilee line to Neasden to see the new head office."

It was only 7 stops on the Jubilee line but a whole world away from St John's Wood. Painter, Pippa and Nick came out of the century-old red brick station to be greeted with the dismal demonstration of what slow decay across decades could do to post war suburbia. Painter checked his phone for messages then followed the map on the screen informing him that their target was only 7 minutes away.

The front elevation of the new building raised Painter's spirits as he acknowledged that the company deserved a medal for improving the local built environment. A more cynical thought then occurred to him; the land would have been dirt cheap and yet close to the important transport link of the North Circular Road that had done so much harm to Neasden by bisecting the original community.

Painter introduced himself to the man behind the desk in reception and was soon rewarded with the rapid approach of a young woman with outstretched hand. The rest of her body could be described as plain, although the smile was warm. The designer silver glasses complemented her light brown hair which had streaks of pink that Painter realised must be chemically induced.

"Welcome, Inspector, to our new head office. My name is Elizabeth and, until the tragic events of yesterday, I was Mr Müller's PA."

At the end of her, no doubt rehearsed, introduction, the voice faltered and Painter realised he had on his hands a fourth woman devoted to serving her now deceased male boss.

"Thank you, Elizabeth. Your building is very impressive and such an improvement on others in this area."

"Absolutely. The company wanted to make a statement when it constructed the building, showing the local people that we're here for the long term and committed to supporting the area. We have 250,000 square feet of modern office space over 7 floors, solar panels on the roof, charging points for electric cars and eco-friendly details like collecting rainwater to flush the loos. Mr Müller was very pleased with how it turned out."

Once again, her voice cracked at the end of a sentence where his name was mentioned.

"I suppose the proximity to the North Circular helped the company decide on the location?"

"Absolutely; access to transport communications was very important for us. The warehouse is immediately behind this building and provides employment for local people. We're getting many applications from staff who previously worked at the depot for the underground service. We aim to be a good employer who brings much needed new opportunities to the area. This is very much part of the rationale behind the company coming to the UK 5 years ago."

"I believe I read in the newspapers that you're an even cheaper rival to the other German discount supermarkets, Lidl and Aldi."

"I think we prefer the term better value," replied Elizabeth with a smile; "I'm sure that's how Mr Müller would have described it."

"May we now see his office?"

"Of course, Inspector; follow me."

A sleek, modern lift took them to the top floor and they walked to a corner office with large glass windows. An estate agent would no doubt have called it a penthouse office although, in reality, the view over the warehouse into the surrounding district was depressing.

"Please tell us exactly what happened yesterday."

"Mr Müller arrived at 9 o'clock as usual after the short walk from the tube station. We quickly went through the work for the day. He delegated some emails for me to answer. He met with the managers of two of the sections within head office and then he left to walk through the warehouse at about 11:30."

"Was that his usual routine?"

"Absolutely; yes, exactly the same every day. After

ensuring that everything was working well in both the office and the warehouse, his habit was to collect his lunch from the canteen and eat it with whoever happened to be at a table with a vacant seat. He felt it provided an opportunity for ordinary members of staff to raise any issues with him informally. However, more senior managers often seemed to arrive for their lunch at the same time, just by coincidence you understand, so I don't think he met that many workers from the coal face."

"Can you give us the names of the people he had lunch with yesterday?"

"Absolutely; yes, Inspector, I can. It's been a subject of discussion that they were some of the last people to see him alive. I'll set up meetings with them for you now, if you like."

"Thank you. Now take your time and think carefully about yesterday. Did anything happen that struck you as being odd or unusual?"

Elizabeth thought for a few moments before replying:

"No, Inspector; yesterday was just like any other day in our office."

"One more question, if I may. Did Mr Müller eat or drink anything during the morning or afternoon?"

"Yes, I made black filter coffee for him and the managers he met at 10 o'clock and the same again for his 3 PM meeting."

"Then please arrange for me to meet with them as

well this morning; I'll use this office if you've no objection."

The first manager to arrive was Stefan who had recently come to the UK from the company's parent in Germany. He confirmed that he drank coffee from the same pot as Mr Müller, the only difference being that Stefan had sugar in his black coffee.

The two managers who shared lunch with Mr Müller described a 15-minute devouring of a pre-packaged sandwich chosen, it seemed, at random from the many displayed in the staff canteen, plus the only food foible Painter could identify. It seemed that Mr Müller was addicted, the exact word used by the manager, to the sweets known as gummy bears. Apparently, German children were given them as a treat and Günter Müller had never grown out of the habit.

Painter informed Elizabeth that a forensic team would visit the office and canteen and he asked her to direct their attention to the sandwiches and packets of gummy bears on sale there. He left Nick and Pippa to get formal statements from the people he'd interviewed and then made his escape from the environs of Neasden, courtesy of the Jubilee line, but not before he'd bought a packet of gummy bears from the canteen and slipped them neatly into the pocket of his suit jacket.

Wednesday 14 October 2020

As Painter ate his cooked breakfast, he checked that the capsule of valsartan that he took daily for his raised blood pressure was smaller than a single gummy bear and could be slipped inside one by making a cut in the side. Smiling to himself, he set off for work, rehearsing the little speech he'd give to the trainees once the bus and tube had delivered him to New Scotland Yard:

"Good morning, everyone. This is a very strange set of cases, because we don't have scenes of crime to work with. We know the means of death but have no suspects. We've no real hint of a motive either. We need to keep working on the only angle we have; that of *opportunity*. Delve deeper into the only people who had the opportunity to slip the poison to each of our victims. I suspect that one or more person in each household or workplace has been recruited by a professional hit man. We've checked their bank accounts and found no new suspicious payments but need to consider that the mastermind who planned all of this may have other ways of giving them money, including cash. Put a track on their bank account to see if there are any large deposits and keep an ear out at their places of work to see if anyone suddenly buys a new sports car. Meanwhile, I need you to find out detailed background on every single person who had opportunity. Where did they go to school? Did they study A level chemistry, which we were told would help them understand how to turn castor beans into ricin poison? Did any of them train in chemistry at university? Divide all these people up between you; go back and interview them again and do full background checks. Nick, check the 2 caterers and 2 packers followed by the 3 car drivers; Pippa, check the 4 cleaning ladies followed by the 4 secretaries. Baako; you can go with Pippa and learn about our ways of working. That's all going to take you time, setting up interviews with 15 people and emailing me your reports as you go along, so we'll meet back here on Friday morning at 08:00 and all consider what you've been able to find out."

As soon as they were out of earshot, Pippa started to grumble to Nick and Baako about Painter:

"He's completely unreasonable, just dumping new work on us to follow up one of his crazy ideas. He's no idea how long all of this takes."

"I know what you mean, Pippa. It's really annoying, but you get used to it after a while and he does get results from his unusual approach."

"I don't know how you put up with it, Nick. He's a terrible sexist, having just allocated most of the women to me and Baako but all the men to you. What do you think, Baako?"

"I'm not the right person to ask about this. I've been

brought up with dominant males who would have a woman taken outside and stoned to death for just speaking her mind or forgetting to wear her hijab. I do find the Inspector to be a bit strange, but perhaps he's not too bad when compared with that behaviour."

Thursday 15 October 2020

Painter poured a large glass of malt and selected a CD by Art Pepper. The glorious alto saxophone filled the study as he thought through what to do next. He hoped that his officers would find a critical new lead but, if they didn't, he needed to identify a new line of investigation they could follow. Aided by the wonderful music, Painter hit upon another potential explanation for the crimes they'd discovered and a way of exploring that possibility.

He bounded down the stairs the next morning, wolfed down the breakfast prepared by Betty and set off for his usual bus and tube journey to New Scotland Yard. Both parts of London Transport performed efficiently so he was in good humour as he greeted his team:

"Right, let's get started. Nick, tell us what you've found out about the people with access to food and present them in the order of the deaths of the 4 cases."

"Before I do that, sir, let me say that Pippa, Baako and I've made a printout of each person for you. We've name, address, date of birth, email address, mobile number, log of recent calls made from phone, log of callers to phone, national insurance number, NHS number, IP address of home computer and browser history. We'll give you just the highlights as we go along. Turning now to the caterer for Case 1, Nicola Jenner is aged 27. She attended Westfield Academy in Watford which is co-educational with 1100 students. Her A levels were in Economics and Biology. She obtained an apprenticeship for a commis chef at Bournemouth for 18 months with a linked job. She then worked in a local hotel for 3 years. After that, she wanted to live in London and applied to work in the Mansion House. This gave her insight into catering in the City of London so, after 2 years, she left to set up her own business. She's single and has lived in the same rented flat in Islington all the time she's been in London."

There were no questions, so Nick continued:

"For Case 2, Mandy Mitchell is aged 28. She went to St Saviours Girls Church of England School in Southwark, near the Elephant and Castle, that has 600 students where she passed A levels in Economics and English. She worked in a restaurant in the Old Kent Road for 3 years and then moved to another restaurant in Barts Square EC1. After 3 more years, she set up her own business supplying catering services to the nearby City of London. She's also single and lives in a flat in the Barbican that she owns courtesy of a large mortgage."

"So; Mandy followed a similar path to Nicola."

"Yes, sir, but the next two are different. For Case 3, we have Brian Richards, aged 20. He attended Muswell Hill Fortismere School, which is co-educational with 1700 students. He only got GCSEs and left to work in the local branch of M&S in Muswell Hill high street as a food packer. He still works there and still lives with his parents in Muswell Hill."

Receiving no comments or questions, Nick continued:

"The food packer for Case 4 is Kevin Jones, aged 29. He went to Harris Academy Peckham. Like Brian Richards, he got GCSEs only. He started work at the local Tesco store in Peckham. After 3 years he moved to Asda in Peckham. After 4 more years, he went to Sainsburys in Peckham where he told me he got good at the computer systems they use. Then, last year, he used his experience to move to this new German supermarket as a senior packer. He's lived in Peckham all his life until he got this latest job when he moved into a rented flat in Neasden. He says it's tiny but big enough for just him."

"Thanks Nick. To summarise for those with access to food, we have two girls who got A levels at school, showed initiative to move away from where they were brought up and eventually went on to start their own small businesses. We then have two boys who didn't do so well academically and worked in local stores. The boy for Case 4 has only now moved on, but he's gained experience by moving around employers in Peckham. None of them got A level chemistry, with Biology being the closest subject. All 4 of them are single. Let's now hear what Pippa has found out about the cleaning ladies."

"Well, sir; for Case 1, you'll remember Mrs Irene Perkins, the rather plump lady of 65. She was brought up in Somerset and only got a few O-levels at school, which I gather was the predecessor to GCSEs. She was a married homemaker with two children but was widowed 8 years ago. She's been with Sir John and Lady Pilkington since they bought the pad in Somerset 5 years ago. She has a pretty good life really, alternating between Somerset and Regents Park. She's driven around in a Rolls Royce and runs the kitchens as she sees fit. I'd be amazed if she did anything to upset the status quo by poisoning her employer."

"There's no accounting for human nature, Pippa. People do the most illogical things if they're riled up. I take your point, but she stays as a suspect for now."

"Then, for Case 2, we have Mrs Violet Jenkins. She's aged 62 and has worked for Lord and Lady Yeast for 8 years. She's lived in Arnos Grove all her life and only got O-levels at school. She's a homemaker who now lives with her husband, their one grown up daughter having moved away. Mrs Jenkins travels to and fro each day to Totteridge on the 251 bus. She seems contented with her life and I got no signal that she was disgruntled with her employer."

There were no comments, so Pippa continued:

"For Case 3, we have Mrs Elsie Williams. You'll remember she had a stooped appearance when we saw her, no doubt from having had a tough life working as a cleaning lady. She's only 67 but looks older. She's worked for Mr and Mrs Randall for 4 years and gave me no complaints. She has an easy commute to Highgate two days a week, coming in on the Northern line from Kentish Town. She's another homemaker, with just a few O-levels to her name, whose two children have flown the nest. She lives there with just her husband who's now retired."

"What was his occupation?"

"I didn't ask that, sir but will find out."

"Please do that, because we'd look pretty foolish if Mr Williams has a degree in chemistry and helped his wife prepare the poison. In fact, both of you should do the same for all the partners of the people on our list."

"Will do, sir. We now move to Case 4, Mrs Patricia Roberts. She's middle aged at 52 but seems younger at heart than the others. She's yet another homemaker but was in the first cohort to take GCSEs when they were introduced. She didn't go on to study at A-level. She's worked for Hannah and Günter Müller for 18 months since they came over from Germany. She likes working for them but says Mrs Müller can be a bit flaky at times, always running off to play tennis. She says the apartment doesn't really need her for 3 days a week but the company's paying, not him personally. Mrs Roberts also has an easy commute, coming in on the Jubilee line from Willesden Green. She lives with her husband and I'll find out what work he does."

"Yes, do that. Also, find out more about what Mrs Roberts meant about the wife being flaky. She might be hinting that you need to dig a bit deeper."

"Will do, sir."

"In summary, we've no suggestion of any motive from these people who had ready access to the food the victims ate. None of them studied chemistry, but we don't know about the 3 of them who have partners. Now let's hear what Nick found out while discussing cars with the 3 drivers."

"For Case 1, sir, we have Albert Harris aged 29. He went to school at Ark Walworth Academy on the Old Kent Road that has a student roll of 1200. He got GCSEs only. He told me he's always loved cars and worked in a local garage to begin with. He then started driving around London aiming to get the knowledge needed to drive a black taxi, but realised things were changing with ready availability of GPS satellite navigation so obtained a private hire licence instead; a process that took him only 4 months. He later completed a drivers' course through the British Chauffeurs Guild. He moved to work for a limousine hire company then replied to an advert placed by Sir John Pilkington. He's single and lives in both Somerset and Regents Park as his employer moves from one place to the other. He seems very contented driving his magnificent Rolls Royce."

"Spare me the comment that you've never travelled in such a car and move on to the next one."

"Yes, sir. For Case 2 we have Eric Evans, aged 26. He went to Broomfield School in Arnos Grove, that has 600 students on the roll, where he only got GCSEs. He became an informal minicab driver, using his own car to do local jobs for cash. Once he turned 21, he joined a proper firm and became a licensed private hire driver following career advice from the Licensed Private Hire Car Association. He's only driven Lord Yeast on one previous occasion. He's married with one small child and lives in Arnos Grove."

"Didn't Arnos Grove crop up somewhere else?"

"Yes, sir; Mrs Violet Jenkins lives there," said Pippa.

"I don't like coincidences, so let's keep track of any that appear, because it might point to links between suspects. Mind you, I have to acknowledge that cleaning ladies and car drivers can't afford houses in Totteridge, so these little people will have to travel from somewhere nearby that's more affordable. Continue, Nick."

"Thank you, sir. For Case 3 we have Tony Baker, aged 25. His story is very similar to that of Eric Evans except that his career advice came from the GMB Union. He attended Acland Burghley School, a mixed comprehensive with 1100 students, in Tufnell Park. He only got GCSEs. He rents a flat in Kentish Town with his girlfriend. He often collects Mr Randall, so would know his routine."

"Thanks Nick. In summary, the 3 drivers are all young men. For Case 2, the driver only took our victim on a single occasion, but the others had regular contact. We need to consider if they could have used this familiarity to get close to the victim and administer the poison, although no ricin was found in any car. We don't have a fourth driver because Case 4 was the only victim to stick to public transport when commuting to work. Let's therefore move to hear what Pippa has found out about the secretaries."

"Thank you, sir. For Case 1, we have Susie Chester, a slim brunette aged 30. She attended Hollyfield School, a co-educational academy, located in Surbiton with 1100 students where she took A levels in English and Drama. She then did a 6 months' secretarial course by distance learning from a group called International Careers, while working at a local branch of Lloyds Bank. After 3 years, she applied to work at the Shell Centre in Lambeth on the South bank as a junior secretary. After 5 more years, she replied to an advert from Raffles Private Equity and went to work in Mayfair. She rents a flat near the Westway flyover with her boyfriend. The other staff in the office speak well of her. For Case 2, we have Carol Wilson, the brunette with designer glasses aged 31 who's a little overweight. She's single and lives in a share house in Whitechapel with three other girls. She went to South Camden Community School, a co-educational comprehensive secondary school in Somers Town where she obtained GCSEs only. She worked for several years as an administrative assistant at a local firm of accountants before being sponsored for an apprenticeship by a bigger local company. This made her eligible to apply to Brewers' Hall who have a scheme for recruiting people schooled in poorer parts of London. She's grateful to the City of London for this opportunity. She's worked for Lord Yeast for 3 years and seems absolutely devoted to him. I'd be surprised if she was prepared to put him in harms' way. I spoke to a couple of girls in the office and they both said she was a lovely person."

"Thanks for that insight. We need to remember that she may have been tricked into administering something that contained the ricin. What about the next one?"

"The PA in Case 3 is called Louise Johnson. Aged 28, she's an attractive, tall, trim blonde. She went to school at Kingsdale Foundation School in Dulwich where she took A level English. She followed a similar route to Susie Chester by doing a 6 months' secretarial course by distance learning, but chose Keystone Courses this time. She joined London Transport as a trainee secretary and worked her way up rapidly through the organisation. She's single and rents a flat in Islington. I had a quiet word with two girls in the office who said that Louise appeared close to her boss. They hinted at a possible personal relationship but had no evidence of this, only a suspicion. They were a bit giggly and I did wonder if they were just jealous of Louise's obvious beauty. Moving on to Case 4, we have Elizabeth Davies. She would be described as plain, with brown hair and glasses. She attended Crest Girls' Academy in Neasden where she passed GCSEs only. She signed up for two secretarial courses, both different from those chosen by Susie Chester and Louise Johnson. She worked as a PA for two local companies that she described as dead end, before jumping at the chance to be the PA to Günter Müller. As we were told, the new supermarket is keen to appoint people from the local community and she's glad of the chance. She has a flat share in Neasden so she can walk to work and describes herself as single at the moment."

"In summary then, none of the 4 secretaries or PAs attended the same place for training. None of them studied chemistry. They all seem to like their current employers. We also have a hint that one of them might like their boss a bit more than required by their job description. In short, we're no further forward in terms of hard facts."

"What do you want us to do next, sir?"

"Follow up on all the outstanding points we've discussed today. Then let's look even deeper into the backgrounds of all these people with opportunity. Check the electoral register, employer files and bank and credit card details for every address every person has ever lived; do they go back a long way? Did they live together in a house share? While you all do that, I'm going to follow up a new line of investigation to consider a new motive: I want to find out who got the jobs vacated by these 4 deaths to see if career ambition might explain why our men were murdered."

* * *

Painter imagined he was taking part in a TV show based on the travelling salesman problem of how to visit 4 places in the shortest possible time. In London, that meant avoiding changing trains wherever possible. He had the classical map of the underground system open on his computer and decided on the optimal route. He'd take the Bakerloo line to Baker Street and walk to Mayfair; walk back to Baker Street for a short trip to Neasden; a long journey on the Jubilee line from there to Stratford; finally, take the Central line to St Pauls. Remarkably, this would allow him to visit all 4 places without having to change once. Hoping his contacts would be free to see him at his preferred times he made a series of calls before leaving his office for Westminster station.

After recovering from the sight of the flamboyant brown and yellow check suit, he learned that the Board of Raffles Private Equity had held an emergency meeting and asked Bertie to act as interim chairman. Painter asked if Bertie had met any of the other 3 victims, but the man denied all knowledge of them.

At Neasden, Painter was shown into the penthouse office recently vacated by Günter Müller to find Stefan ensconced behind the desk, looking very much at home. Stefan explained that the arrangement was only temporary while Germany decided whether to send a permanent replacement. He had never come across any of the other 3 people Painter mentioned.

At Stratford, Painter found that the deputy to William Randall was acting up on a temporary basis. When questioned, he admitted that he would be applying for the permanent post when it was advertised. He denied any knowledge of the other 3 victims.

In the City, Painter found that the standard practice had been followed; the senior non-executive director was acting up until the Board made a permanent appointment. The man admitted that, out of a sense of duty to the company, he would let his name go forward for consideration for the definitive post but denied knowledge of any of the other 3 people.

The travelling salesman game was complete once Painter retraced his steps to St Pauls and let the Central line take him to Mile End to catch his bus home.

∞

Monday 19 October 2020

It didn't seem long before Painter had to make the bus journey in reverse; 277 to Mile End followed by the District line to Westminster from where he walked for just two minutes to reach New Scotland Yard.

"Tell me what you've all found out."

"We've identified all the details of the 6 husbands, wives and partners of the people we discussed. Full details are in your folder but, in summary, none of them studied chemistry and they all have, or had before they retired, routine jobs like shop assistant, bank teller, bricklayer, shelf stacker in a supermarket."

"That doesn't sound very interesting, Nick, but thanks for finding it all out. What about you, Pippa?"

"You were right about Mrs Roberts, sir; I got some good gossip out of her. She became suspicious when Mrs Müller started touching up her makeup before going off to play tennis at the nearby club in Regent's Park."

"Where exactly in the park?"

Pippa consulted her notes.

"It's off the Inner Circle, near York Bridge, sir."

"That's close to Ulster Terrace," exclaimed Painter. "We should consider if there's a link between cases 4 and 1. I wonder if Lady Pilkington plays tennis?"

"I doubt if she's into Mrs Müller's game, sir. Mrs Roberts said Hannah reminded her of how her teenage daughter behaved before going out on a date. I looked on Facebook and there are plenty of comments about the services available from the young, handsome tennis coaches."

"Well, well. I think you and I should go and see Mrs Müller and find out what's been going on. Set up an appointment please at her house at a time when the cleaning lady won't be there."

"Yes, sir."

"What else have you got?"

"Well sir, I took on the task of listing all the places our people of interest lived or worked because I thought it would improve my knowledge of the geography of London. We used the electoral register and bank records as you suggested. All the details are in your folder, but I think the map shows us three areas of interest."

They all moved into a huddle to stare at Pippa's iPad.

"I left out Bournemouth and Somerset, which was where two people grew up, to get the scale right. You'll see we have a cluster in northwest London around Neasden and Arnos Grove, another in South London around the Old Kent Road and a third around the City of London."

"What do the colours represent?"

"Green is where they went to school, blue is where they worked in the past, yellow is where they work now and pink is where they live now. The 4 red pins represent where our victims were taken ill."

"This is good work, Pippa, but what do the 3 clusters mean? It could just be where cheap accommodation is available for people who work in places like Mayfair."

"They could be groups of people who belong to the same extended family, or they could be business associates. I've seen these links many times when making judgements about criminals in Afghanistan."

"I agree that's possible in theory, Baako, but the problem is we've found no links between any of these people. However, we've no other ideas, so feel free to check again and dig deep to see if you can identify any connections between even two people in these groups."

For the benefit of Pippa and Baako, Painter then told them about the travelling salesman problem and how he'd managed to visit 4 distinct sites in London without having to change underground trains on a single occasion. He then told them what he'd learned:

"All 4 of them said they'd reluctantly stepped into the shoes of the recently departed but they all looked as if they were enjoying their new positions. To run through them in the order of the cases, rather than in the order I saw them, I still believe Bertie is genuinely saddened by the death of his old school friend. However, private capital works in a ruthless world and Bertie wouldn't have survived if he didn't have a strong streak of competitiveness.

He must remain on our list of suspects. The same applies for the brewer, although I had the impression that the senior non-executive director had been looking forward to retirement, so is a less strong candidate for murder. In contrast, the deputy to William Randall is still young and thrusting, so I could see his ambition driving him to want the top job. Whether that ambition was enough to make him commit murder is another question. I got the same impression about Stefan at the Neasden headquarters; he looked very comfortable behind that desk. However, he expected a replacement to be sent from Germany so must have known that murdering his colleague would not lead to a permanent position. In summary, power is a powerful force, as illustrated by the list of poisonings in literature that Pippa prepared, but I didn't get an overwhelming impression that these people were sufficiently driven to commit murder. Finally, this avenue of investigation requires that all 4 of them conspired together to get rid of their senior colleagues, but they all denied knowledge of the other victims. Your job now is to check to see if they were telling the truth. Is there any link, based on family, business, school, social activities or sport between these men? If you told me tomorrow that all 4 of them play golf together, you'd make me a very happy man."

* * *

Painter poured himself a large glass of malt and looked to see which jazz artist might get his little grey cells working overtime to think about the ways people could meet up informally. When he saw the CD by Bix Beiderbecke, he imagined a smoky, cosy club in the 1920s where a conspiracy between mafiosi could easily be hatched. When he saw that the name of the first track was called *The Connection*, his mind was made up and he settled into the comfortable chair in his den to listen to the dramatic cornet playing.

He'd originally imagined that a grand conspirator had contacted 4 secretaries or 4 caterers or 4 housekeepers and bribed them to poison items of food. This mastermind could have identified his stooges through secretarial colleges, catering schools or agencies employing cleaning ladies. Yet, Painter's investigations had shown that none of the people with opportunity had trained or worked together. He now needed to re-orientate his idea of a mastermind linked to the perpetrators by geography rather than occupation.

If Neasden/ Arnos Grove was the focus, the group would include nobody for Case 1, Violet Jenkins and Eric Evans for Case 2, no-one for Case 3, Elizabeth Davies and Kevin Jones for Case 4. To bring in a candidate for Case 1, he would have to accept Islington, where Nicola Jenner lived, although Google said it was 6 miles from Arnos Grove. To have a candidate for Case 3 he would need to accept Kentish Town, Tufnell Park or Muswell Hill, 5 miles, 5 miles and 3 miles away respectively, to bring in Elsie Williams, Tony Baker and Brian Richards. If he was going to accept a distance of 6 miles for Islington, then Willesden Green was only 8 miles from Arnos Grove which would add Patricia Roberts to the list.

If the Old Kent Road was the base, then the following would be involved: Albert Harris for Case 1, Mandy Mitchell for Case 2, no-one for Case 3 and Kevin Jones for Case 4. Google told him it was only 3.5 miles from Dulwich to the Old Kent Road so he could potentially include Louise Johnson for Case 3.

If the City was where the conspirators belonged, then he'd have to look into Nicola Jenner for Case 1, Mandy Mitchell and Carol Wilson for Case 2, Somers Town being only 2 miles away from St Paul's cathedral. There was no-one obvious for Case 3, although Kentish Town and Tufnell Park were each only 3.5 miles from St Paul's, potentially bringing in Elsie Williams and Tony Baker respectively. For Case 4, he could find no plausible connection to the City.

After a refill of malt and another CD by Bix, Painter's thought experiment was beginning to put limits on the number of interactions between the many people in the 4 cases. He needed to remember that distance wasn't always an accurate guide to easy accessibility between people in London and use his knowledge of local geography and transport connections if some cases became linked. The information available so far suggested that he should deploy his limited resources around the Old Kent Road, which looked to be the best option because there was a candidate from each of the 4 cases.

He then began to worry about whether any of these possible connections would provide real leads in these mysterious cases. Painter had to admit that he was not yet on top of what was going on. He found his mind wandering and he couldn't settle down to think it all through any more. If he was to get any refreshing sleep tonight, he'd need to choose a different type of jazz and reach for his special bottle of 16-year-old malt. The fiery, peaty flavour of Lagavulin from the Isle of Islay warmed his gullet as Jacques Loussier played Bach to act as a lullaby to soothe his troubled mind.

Tuesday 20 October 2020

They left the tube train at St John's Wood and walked the short distance to their destination. Painter led Pippa towards the entrance to the apartments, showed his warrant card and was directed to the flat he'd visited one time before which contained the elegant but spartan Scandinavian furniture. Hannah Müller let him in and, with her perfect English spoken with a German accent, offered refreshments which Painter declined.

"Have you got information about what happened to my husband, Inspector?"

"I'm afraid I don't, although I have a few questions I need to put to you. I apologise in advance if they're personal in nature, but you'll appreciate that I need to investigate all leads we get in a case."

"Of course, Inspector; how can I help?"

"My Sergeant routinely follows up all information we receive during the course of an investigation. I understand you go regularly to play tennis at a club in Regent's Park."

"Yes, that's correct."

"Have you ever met there someone called Lady Pilkington who lives in Ulster Terrace just round the corner from the club?"

"No, I don't remember that name."

"Very well. Do you have tennis lessons there?"

"Yes, I do. My backhand is improving very much as a result."

"My Sergeant also found out through social media that the club has quite a reputation for close friendships between those paying for lessons and those doing the teaching. Can I ask if tennis was the only game you played when going repeatedly to Regent's Park?"

"I'm not quite sure I understand what you're asking me, Inspector."

"Then let me put it another way; were you friendly with one of the tennis coaches?"

"Yes, I get on very well with the young man who teaches me regularly."

"How would you describe your relationship with him?"

"Coach and trainee would describe it well."

"I'm sure, but was there more to it than that?"

"What exactly are you asking me, Inspector?"

"I'm asking if there was a romantic element to your relationship?"

Mrs Müller swallowed hard before replying:

"Are you sure I can't get you some refreshments, Inspector?"

"Nothing for me, thank you, although I would like an honest answer to my direct question."

Mrs Müller smiled at Painter and began to talk with smooth, Germanic efficiency:

"Let me explain the background, Inspector. My husband and I came here about 18 months ago. He was very pleased to have this promotion and I supported him 100%. While he was busy at work, I did as much as I could to provide him with a comfortable home to come back to at the end of a long day. I think the painters and decorators were here when you came before. That's their fourth visit and the apartment is now fully redecorated. I've also bought all new furniture in a style to please him. However, I've also become bored. We're here for my husband's work and have little time to meet people and socialise. I began to feel trapped in this beautiful cage. To make friends, I joined the tennis club and have felt much better since I did so."

"I'm sure you have Mrs Müller, but I still need to ask if your friendship at the club had a romantic element?"

Hannah looked to be losing some of her confidence:

"Is this line of questioning really necessary, inspector?"

"Yes, I'm afraid it is, Mrs Müller. Please tell me clearly if you were romantically involved with your tennis coach."

Hannah swallowed hard before replying:

"The relationship did develop in that direction."

"Are we talking about a full sexual relationship?"

"Is it required in Britain to describe these things in such a way?"

"Indeed, it is, Mrs Müller, but let me make the process

easier for you. I put it to you that you were having a sexual relationship with this man. Just nod if that's correct."

The cool, collected Teutonic persona disappeared as Hannah Müller stared between the beautifully laid grey carpet and the elegant Scandinavian furniture as she gave the required nod.

"Thank you for confirming that. I now need to explain why this information is relevant to our enquiry. We often find that people are murdered by their spouse. Did you kill, or arrange to have killed, Günter Müller?"

Hannah Müller looked up from the carpet, horrified.

"Of course not! I loved my husband and did everything I could to help him and his career. This other business was just a bit of fun to while away the time. I'm still young you know and not unattractive. It was flattering to have another man, a younger one, paying attention to me. I know it was foolish but was perhaps my last chance to enjoy life on my own terms before returning to Germany at the end of my husband's posting."

"I can see how the relationship became established but need to consider whether you might have wished to see your husband out of the picture so you could focus your attentions on this young, athletic man."

"How could you think such a terrible thing? I loved my husband and this other business was just what you British call a fling. I was supporting Günter's career while maintaining my needs for companionship."

"I need a yes or no answer to this final question; did you or your tennis coach kill your husband?"

"No."

The room seemed to have got colder over the 20 minutes since Painter and Pippa had walked through the door.

"Thank you for answering my questions today. I apologised earlier for their personal nature and do so again now. I hope you understand that it was necessary to define exactly the nature of your relationship. I'll need you to give me the name and contact details of this tennis coach. Sergeant Trelawny here will now get a statement from him and will return tomorrow to get you to sign a written summary of what was said today. I will compare those documents and decide if the information is relevant to the murder of your husband. It may be necessary to ask you further questions. If so, I will invite you to come to New Scotland Yard and would advise you to bring a solicitor."

* * *

Painter needed advice and he knew exactly the right person to ask. Before picking up the phone he considered where they should meet. New Scotland Yard would be too formal and she would probably submit an invoice. The pub would be ideal and they could sit outside to avoid their conversation being overheard. He should definitely resist any attempts from her to invite him back to her narrowboat lest she tried to seduce him as she had done successfully on a previous occasion. Having set his ground rules and red lines, Painter dialled the number and looked forward to benefitting from her expertise that evening.

* * *

"Hello Ruth. Why don't you grab that table over there out of the way and I'll go to the bar."

He soon returned with her standard tipple of draft cider plus a pint of bitter for himself. They huddled together across the table as he told his story in a conspiratorial whisper and eventually leaned back to hear her opinion.

"This is a complicated subject that'll need at least one more pint if I'm to do it justice."

When Painter returned from the bar, Ruth gave her opinion.

"You could be right about a controlling mastermind from the underworld paying or tricking 4 different people to administer poison. Yet, you've given me no sense of why these fine, upstanding, ordinary members of the public would agree to do such a thing. It's possible, but, unless he or she offered a very large sum of money, I can't see them signing up to the plan. The psychology's all wrong."

"Do you have an alternative explanation?"

"Yes; you might not need to invoke a mastermind. What if 4 of these people agreed to work as a self-organised group to achieve a specific objective that we've no understanding of yet?"

"You mean like the Three Musketeers?"

"Perhaps, although there were 4 musketeers in the end, just like your 4 imagined murderers. They're a possible model to consider but I was thinking more of a bond that was established between 4 people long ago during the formative years of pre-adolescent or adolescent childhood. Think of the Famous Five books by Enid Blyton."

"I hadn't considered that sort of link. Thanks Ruth; I'll keep my eye open for a suspect with a dog called Timmy from now on."

Wednesday 21 October 2020

Sitting in the upper deck of the 277, Painter decided it was time to activate the next step in the investigation once he'd received a progress report.

He started by telling the others what he and Pippa had learned about Hannah and the tennis coach:

"Their statements match up, so I'm inclined to think that this is an incidental finding, not relevant to our murders. The coach clearly indicated that the relationship was just a short-term fling and that he was also involved with another woman from the tennis group. That means it doesn't fit the pattern of two people planning to run away together who are prepared to kill anyone who stands in their way. Do you agree, Pippa?"

"Yes, sir, I do."

"Moving on to Nick, tell me what you've managed to find out between you."

"We obtained copies of the CVs of the four people who were promoted as a result of the deaths, sir. We interviewed them and the people who work in their offices to identify hobbies and sports. We did an extensive trawl of social media for each of them and I must tell you that Baako is getting good at that aspect of our work. However, we can't find a single link between any of them. Specifically, none of them plays golf; all the details are in the file, but Bertie plays croquet, Stefan plays squash, the man at London Transport goes to a gym while the brewer's only sport is playing bridge.

"That's a shame, but thanks for excluding the possibility. They always looked like an odd set to be friends, but the same could be said for many of the people who had the opportunity to commit these crimes."

"What's our next move, sir?"

"Let's now try something different, Pippa. We've imagined that some mastermind recruited at least 4 people, one of whom had close contact with each of our 4 victims. We've assumed this recruitment happened recently, but what if it took place many years ago? When I mentioned this before, you brought up the analogy of sleepers in spy novels put into position years before they were needed. Leaving aside why any such plan should be activated now, let's see if there's any connection between our people with opportunity when we look back further into their lives. We've considered their schools to see what qualifications they got, hoping to see A level chemistry, but what about primary schools and where they lived then? Go back in time to find out all about their early lives, their families, where they were born, who they went to school with. I know it's more difficult than tracking adults through the electoral register, HMRC and employers, so I'll give you two days to complete the tasks, meeting back here at 15:00 on Friday. I suggest you start by interviewing each of the people again and asking where and when they were born so we can see who's listed on their birth certificates."

"Will do, sir, but if they go back a long way, why aren't any of them listed as contacts on their phones?"

"Good question, Pippa. I don't know the answer, but it does suggest another specific question you could ask them: **do you use a mobile phone other than the one you gave us the details of?** If they really are sleepers, they won't tell you now about any burner phone, but that will give us a definite lie they've told which we can present when we bring them to court. It may even make one of them panic and call one of the others, so monitor their phone records. And have no doubt about it; we're pretty confused at the moment about what's going on here, but I will bring clarity through our careful investigations and will bring these bastards to face justice in the end."

∞

Friday 23 October 2020

Painter went to his office at the allotted time to find Nick, Pippa and Baako standing outside like dogs straining at leashes.

"Looks like you've got something to tell me."

"Yes, sir;" they all chimed at once. "We've gone back to primary school level and childhood addresses and have what looks to be a great lead. Four of the 15 suspects with opportunity attended the same school."

The hairs stood to attention on the back of Painter's neck as he realised this could be a major breakthrough in the mystifying case.

"Which school?" he asked quietly.

"Ivydale School, Ivydale Road, Nunhead, sir," replied Nick. "School records give 4 addresses that are very close to each other. I don't know the place myself, but Nunhead Cemetery seems to be the nearest geographical feature."

"That's one of the Magnificent Seven private cemeteries set up in the early 1800s but now neglected, like the more famous Highgate. They were all built on wonderful open land on what was once the edge of the city but are now a bit spooky with many graves in poor condition and rats running around."

"I still don't understand why we didn't find phone connections between these 4 people."

"As I said, Pippa, they may have burner phones that we're unaware of. Alternatively, they may have taken the precaution of avoiding all telecommunications by simply meeting up at one of the houses or even Nunhead Cemetery to discuss their plans in person. They may have been doing this since childhood so it would come naturally to them. Imagine those books written by Enid Blyton about the escapades of the Famous Five."

"I don't remember those children turning into serial killers."

"I agree, Pippa, but think of the model for now until we get to understand their motive. You've all done great work to give us our first real lead. Now go to the electoral register and find out who lives at those 4 addresses at the moment or has done so in the past."

Monday 26 October 2020

It was good to see his officers fired up as they gave their reports at the morning meeting:

"We've got some really interesting information for you, sir about deaths from Covid. Baako has created family trees for the 4 families of interest, so I'll let her talk you through it."

"Thanks Pippa; sounds intriguing."

"To begin with I should say, Inspector Painter, that our investigations are not yet complete and we do know of one other death from Covid in families of the 15 suspects, but I'll concentrate for now on the 4 families where one of the members attended the primary school in Nunhead. I'll present the families in the order in which someone died.

"Thanks, Baako; go ahead, I'm all ears."

"The first death was of Albert Harris aged 81 who, confusingly, has the same first name as his grandson who was the chauffeur in Case 1. Albert senior had lived all his life in the family house in Nunhead but was not in good health latterly. They moved him in September 2019 into a care home in Peckham. The first wave of Covid cases brought the virus into the facility and Albert was one of 4 residents to die. The second person to die from Covid at the age of 56 was Mrs Margaret Jones, the mother of

Kevin Jones, the food packer in Case 4. The third person to die from Covid was Mr Peter Johnson, the 55-year-old father of Louise the secretary in Case 3. The fourth one was only 33 years old, but she had serious medical problems that put her at risk of dying from Covid. Evie Potter was the sister of Mandy Mitchell, the caterer in Case 2. She has a different surname from her sister because she's married. All the other 3 people have the same surnames as our suspects."

"This is good work from all of you. Our case is firming up now and I'm beginning to see what might have happened. These 4 people were members of families that were close to each other, emotionally as well as geographically. They might have formed a little gang when they were kids, like the Famous Five that the profiler suggested to me. Let's call them the Fatal Four for now. When they lost not just one but 4 close relatives, they all met up again and decided to take action and kill our 4 victims. But what I don't yet understand is why they chose them? Find out all you can about these 4 families, particularly the 4 people who died from Covid. I can see why the appearance of the pandemic might have upset our 4 suspects and brought them together but can't see why they chose our 4 victims. I also need you to find factual information that puts our suspects at important places as we build our case. You've got the dates of death but now find out the dates of the funerals. Can we place our 4 suspects at any of the funerals? If we can, we can make the case that they had the opportunity to conspire to commit these murders. In my day, we used to look through the descriptions in the local paper that listed the main mourners; they also used to state who gave the eulogy. I'm not sure they send out journalists to do that any more, but see what you can find out. Try to find a book of condolence for each funeral and see who signed it. That might be in the hands of the family, but the funeral director will have kept a list of money donated in memory of the deceased. Also, check the credit cards of our 4 suspects to see if they bought train or bus tickets on the days of the funerals."

Tuesday 27 October 2020

His officers weren't so fired up this morning, instead looking rather tired as they gave their reports:

"We've got more details about the funerals, sir. All took place at the same church in Nunhead that has an unusual name and backstory. It's the *Church of St Antony with St Silas* and was consecrated in April 2003 after the previous church of St Silas had been demolished and the church of St Antony was sold. The funerals all took place in the order that the 4 people died, with none being delayed. All 4 had the same vicar and were managed by the same firm of funeral directors. We spoke to the owner of the funeral company who knows his locals well. He's given us all the background information so far. You were correct that each book of condolence was given back to each family. You were also right about the list of financial donations; all 4 of our suspects were listed in the records. Also, each of them used their credit card to buy a rail ticket to Nunhead or Peckham Rye stations on the days of the funerals."

"This is all good news. It adds to the body of evidence showing that our 4 suspects probably attended all 4 funerals. However, it's only circumstantial evidence that needs to be backed up when we're ready to interview people. The suspects may admit that they attended and/or other family members may state that they were present. We'll need such hard, factual, confirmed evidence to build a case against them. Now, what more have you found out about the 4 family members who died? Give me the information in order of their relevance to our cases."

"For Case 1 we have Albert Harris senior aged 81, the grandfather of Albert Harris the chauffeur. He died in a care home nearby in Peckham. He'd worked all his life as a painter and decorator and lived at number 178 Ivydale Road all his adult life. For Case 2 we have Evie Potter aged 33, the sister of Mandy Mitchell the caterer. Both sisters were brought up in number 180 Ivydale Road. Evie worked as a barmaid in a pub in Peckham. For Case 3 we have Peter Johnson aged 55, the father of Louise Johnson the secretary. He lived in number 184 Ivydale Road and worked all his life as a bus driver."

"Hold on a minute. Which bus company did he work for?"

"I didn't ask that, sir."

"Well go back and ask now. Don't you see? If he worked for London Transport that gives us a link to one of our 4 victims. Not only that, the victim in the same Case 3 was William Randall who also worked for London Transport. It's a tenuous link, because lots of people in London must be employed by London Transport, but we need to follow it up."

"Will do, sir. Now, for Case 4, we have Margaret

Jones aged 56, the mother of Kevin Jones the packer. She was a check-out worker at a supermarket in Peckham."

"Which supermarket?"

"I didn't get that information, sir."

"Well, you know what you have to do now, don't you? If the supermarket belonged to this new company from Germany, we'd have a link to a second case. Indeed, that victim was Günter Müller, case number 4. I don't want to get carried away with too much speculation, but I predict the other 2 will have connections to Raffles Private Equity and to the brewer. Hold on; didn't you say that Evie Potter for Case 2 worked as a barmaid? Go and find out which brewery owns the pub. Now, for Case 1 we just need to find a link with Raffles Private Equity. At our first meeting, Bertie told me the sort of businesses they were involved with, so let me thumb through my notes. Here it is; no painters and decorators mentioned, but they do own care homes. Find out if the last pillow on which Albert Harris senior rested his head was owned by Raffles."

* * *

With a pint of cider in one hand and a pint of bitter in the other, Painter made his way to the isolated outdoor seat in the pub.

He started by telling Ruth how the investigations had

identified 4 individuals connected with each other since childhood and shared his moniker of the Fatal Four. After giving her all the details, he asked for her profiler's experience of what might have motivated them.

"I wonder if they saw themselves as avengers doing their bit. They may have acted in the past as a group of children to take on projects, so a new one presented itself to them as adults. They may have thought of themselves as heroes, going out to right wrongs. Remember what Bertolt Brecht says about them; **Happy is the land that has no need of heroes**. The major psychological event here is the death of 4 loved people from Covid. This could trigger them to reform their team to get back at people who are tenuously linked to the pandemic that killed their relatives. There might also be a component of class warfare here; hitting back at the managers who are able to work on Zoom while leaving the little people to get exposed to the virus. Those stalwarts called key workers expected a redrafting of the social contract once the pandemic was over, encouraged by Boris saying we're all in it together. Instead, the social solidarity proclaimed so loudly in the heat of the pandemic vanished as soon as a vaccine was discovered. These people need to be treated with dignity and respect, or paid danger money. The psychologist Ken Doka called this *disenfranchised grief* because the cause of death is so politically toxic that it can't be mentioned in polite company. We have the same problem with AIDS and with suicide. I'll send you a link to a book written between the wars by RH Tawney, a Christian lecturer in economics with a socialist perspective. He said that creating equality of opportunity was only a partial step towards what a society needs. He talked about *equality of condition* which meant that people got equal respect if they contributed to society as well as they possibly could. Individuals could then hold their heads up high, just as people with technical skills do in modern Germany, safe in the knowledge that they're members of the community respected as much as those of us with university degrees."

"Would that be sufficient to turn 4 citizens without police records into serial killers?"

"Let's see now. We're all just one step away from a downward spiral, triggered by prosaic life events such as career disappointment or romantic failure. As Shakespeare says in Hamlet:

"To be, or not to be, that is the question:
Whether 'tis nobler in the mind to suffer
The slings and arrows of outrageous fortune,
Or to take Arms against a Sea of troubles,
And by opposing end them: to die, to sleep."

Here, Hamlet is contemplating suicide to escape the daily tribulations of life, but it works for murder as well.

For a more contemporary slant on murder, a character in a recent film says: **all it takes to commit murder is a bad day and the right victim**. Here, you have an accumulation of bad days."

"You mean the pressures and insults of being little people built up until one of them cracked and the others followed?"

"That's right, although you're considering each person as an individual. We should also review and incorporate the psychological significance of each insult for the whole group. You've told me that the first death was of Albert Harris. He was the grandfather of young Albert, but was he a grandfather figure to them all? The second death was Margaret Jones, mother of Kevin, but did she mother them all while they were growing up? Likewise, was Peter Johnson a father figure to the whole group as well as being the biological father of Louise? The last death was Evie Potter, the sister of Mandy Mitchell. As well as being a sister, her age suggests she could have been a member of the original group. In other words, you perhaps should be thinking of the Fatal Five rather than the Fatal Four. A loss of one of their members at a tragically early age could be the last straw that pushed them to avenge all the deaths. So, in answer to your question, I don't see why these tragic deaths couldn't turn these upright citizens into serial killers. Never underestimate the cumulative effect of repeated psychological trauma.

Of course, this is only an interpretation of the facts, but it may help focus your investigations."

"Thanks, Ruth, for that amazing insight. One more question; why would they choose these 4 victims in particular?"

"It may just have been the convenience of having access to them. Kill the head of London Transport as a representative of all the managers on the underground and buses. I can't imagine that their plan went back further in time because no-one knew the virus was on its way. How do you think they got close enough to their targets to poison them?"

"We don't know until they make their confessions but can hazard a few guesses from the only times they had opportunity. For Case 1, the driver must have given Sir John some food or drink during the car journey to Mayfair. His PA told me they used to serve cakes at board meetings until Lady Pilkington put a stop to them 6 months ago to help control her husband's weight. It would be easy for Albert to have conspired with Sir John to provide a piece of cake on each morning trip to Mayfair only to give him a poisoned one on the fateful day. He probably provided a plate to catch the crumbs as a way of reducing our chance of detecting poison, especially after he'd given the roller a good valeting. No-one would regard a chauffeur cleaning out a car as anything suspicious, so I suppose the driver took the lowest personal risk of the 4 of them, although he's probably lost the job he loved. For Case 2, the caterer must have poisoned a specific item of food that she placed in front of Lord Yeast. For Case 3, the PA is particularly attractive and we got a hint of gossip that she might be having an affair with her boss, so I imagine she seduced him and rewarded him afterwards with a food item."

"She may have noticed his roving eye and decided to encourage him once the group's plan was set. If she volunteered to give her body to the cause, it would have encouraged the others to sign up to make sacrifices as well."

"The packer in Case 4 presumably befriended his target by offering him a gummy bear when he was walking around the warehouse or when he met staff at lunchtime in the canteen. It was a subject of common gossip that the boss was addicted to these things, so it wouldn't be difficult to get him to accept a poisoned one."

"Who do you think took a leading role by volunteering to produce the batch of poison that they all used."

"I don't know, but the caterer's the obvious first choice so that's where I'll look."

Wednesday 28 October 2020

Painter settled into his seat at Blackfriars station and waited for the train to depart. The first stop was Elephant and Castle where one of the many dreadful blocks of social housing flats, built in the 1960s to great acclaim, was now being demolished at the edge of the station. The solidly built Victorian terraces surrounding this monstrosity were still standing despite being built more than a century earlier. His taxpayer's blood boiled at the dreadful waste of public money these demolitions represented as well as the generations of children brought up in appalling circumstances to join the criminal underclass. His mood improved as the train took him away from this classic example of how society shat from a great height onto the little people. He saw much better housing at Denmark Hill as well as the forked ends of the Victorian wards that comprised King's College Hospital which were still in use today. The housing at Peckham Rye and then Nunhead was still basically refurbished Victorian terraces but looked to be in excellent condition from his vantage point.

A gentle walk uphill from Nunhead station took him directly to Ivydale Road. He walked along the entire length of the straight road, noticing the voices of young children on the left coming presumably from a nursery school hidden behind the houses. On both sides of the road ran uninterrupted terraces of mid-Victorian era, punctuated by occasional pairs or trios of more modern replacements that filled the gaps created 80 years ago by the Luftwaffe. He located numbers 178, 180, 184 and 186 on the right-hand side, noting that their back gardens must abut the cemetery. His walk stopped when a road appeared on the right, presumably marking the boundary of the cemetery. Rejecting the delights of the pub opposite, Painter continued walking forward until he reached the Church of St Antony with St Silas which was too modern for his liking. He saw an elderly gentleman in the grounds and struck up a conversation. It seemed that the original church had suffered from subsidence. This new one was built on the same land but with better foundations. It had excellent facilities for the local community, but the parishioner missed the old church and the sermons of the previous vicar who preached an eye for an eye every Sunday. Having confirmed that the dates of such fire and brimstone sermons included the formative years of the Fatal Five, Painter retraced his steps along Ivydale Road, taking time to note the obvious signs of gentrification, including a workman on scaffolding refurbishing the original Victorian plaster casts on the front elevation. Neighbouring houses had scaffolding up to support the modern equivalent of adding value to a house; installation of loft conversions or solar panels.

At the end of Ivydale Road he turned left, instead

of going the last hundred yards down to the station and searched for the entrance to the cemetery. It was obvious that the place had been neglected since the 1960s when the cemetery became full and could provide no further income for the owners, but he still found some fine examples of Victorian graveyard art. He chose a path that clung to the left-hand side of the site which he was sure must run alongside Ivydale Road. The trees were thick and overgrown, but he could see the rear elevations of an occasional terraced house. From time to time, a narrow dirt pathway led to the back of a property through a gate. As if on cue, Painter heard voices of children, older than those in the nursery school, playing games behind one such gate. He imagined the Fatal Five following this time-worn ritual of childhood, including creating and maintaining some of the pathways with their small feet as they crept out into the cemetery to begin their next adventure. The area was pleasant now in daytime, but did those children also venture out at dusk? Did these scary experiences build camaraderie and allegiance among them? Could they recently have drawn upon this old alliance of friendships to join forces in a project to kill 4 upright citizens? Mystic Meg clearly thought so.

Painter found a pathway where he could hear the distant sounds of younger children at play. Having thereby located the position of the nursery school, he moved further down to find several pathways any one of which would give access to numbers 178-186. As he came back onto the main track, he saw a woman feeding a blackbird that appeared almost tame. Further on, he saw a woman pushing a baby in a pram and a man walking a dog. This was no longer a scary place and potential site of planning a major crime, but a resource used by many locals for recreation without fear. Near the exit opposite where he had entered the cemetery, he saw an elderly woman sitting in quiet contemplation before a grey, granite memorial to those who died in the 1914-1918 war. From her age, Painter assumed she was thinking of her father.

As he walked through the ornate iron gates the sun was no longer hidden by the trees and Painter felt his mood lift. He turned left to soon find the pub he had rejected when he first found it. Now he had completed his reconnoitre of the area he could justify a reward. The pub menu in the Waverley Arms confirmed his impression that Ivydale Road was a middle-class enclave in London; grilled halloumi with beetroot humus topped with sweet potato crisps was not a traditional British dish. He ordered sausages with mashed potatoes and onion gravy. After washing the main course down with a pint of real ale he succumbed to apple crumble topped with vanilla ice cream. His promise to the GP to lose weight would have to wait another day.

Thursday 29 October 2020

"Good morning, everyone; tell me what you've managed to find out."

"All the details are in the file, sir but, in summary, it's all as you suspected. For Case 1, the care home where Albert Harris died is owned ultimately by Raffles Private Equity. For Case 2, Evie Potter the barmaid was employed in a pub owned by Lord Yeast's brewery. For Case 3, Peter Johnson did drive a bus for London Transport. For Case 4, the branch where Margaret Jones worked at check-out is owned by the new German supermarket chain."

"Excellent news. We're making progress now from the application of basic plodding police work and everything's starting to fit together. These 4 deaths don't seem so mysterious now that we know the connection between them. While you were finding out those key facts, I went to see Mystic Meg again."

Noticing the blank look on Baako's face, Painter explained:

"Our profiler's name is Ruth, but I call her Mystic Meg because of her ability to see things that are invisible to us, just like the famous TV psychic. Well, she's come up trumps once again. She agrees it's likely that the 4 of them were in a group or club during their formative years. And, get this, she thinks that Evie Potter was also in the group, so we really are dealing with the Famous Five, which we're now calling the Fatal Five. Meg thinks there are two forces that could have combined to turn them into killers. The first was the progressive loss of loved ones from within the extended family. The second was class envy. These are all little people; essential workers during Covid but poorly paid and poorly protected. They aimed to get back at those fat cats they blamed for failing to protect staff at the sharp end. The final insult was the loss of Evie Potter, one of their own. This stimulated the group to form their plan by hitting back at whoever they had contact with. Ruth suggests that Louise Johnson set an example of the sacrifices necessary by giving her body to gain access to William Randall. The others then felt obliged to take risks with their contacts. I went to Nunhead yesterday and located the houses where they were all brought up. The houses back onto Nunhead Cemetery and I could imagine a group of kids forming allegiances there. The local church is modern, but they would have been preached to by the old vicar in an old church with stories of an eye for an eye. When we get to the interview stage, I plan to ask them specifically if they went to that church. However, before we get there, we need hard evidence because everything so far is circumstantial. Although I believe we now have their plan, we need to work out how to catch them and bring them to book."

* * *

The large hand of the clock was approaching the vertical position, so Painter started his walk upstairs in response to the summons from *she who must be obeyed*. He was glad he had real progress to report and looked forward to her complimenting him on bringing order to chaos. He was shown straight in by the PA, turned right at the framed degree certificate and began his briefing for Veronica. After 10 minutes, he summed up and explained why he needed search warrants.

Veronica sat, motionless, in stunned silence. After a few seconds she slowly got up and looked pensively out the window at the grey London skies.

"Is that it?" she said calmly. "Is that really all you've got?"

"Veronica this is a promising lead..."

"Promising lead? Promising lead!" she said, losing her cool. "We've got four murders in London and all you've got is four people who went to the same school and lived vaguely near each other 25 years ago! You don't know if they've even met each other apart from at recent funerals! Have you heard of the 6 degrees of separation? I could link you with a monk in Tibet if I looked hard enough!

You have no phone records, no text messages and no social media posts between them. You've got no idea where they made the poison or how they administered it. You don't even know why they used poison and you've got a flimsy motive at best!"

Painter's blood was boiling. How dare she talk to him like that? He jumped to his feet, his chair clattering to the floor behind him.

"I've got 25 years of intuition telling me this is the case!"

"I've had enough of your intuition Painter! This is the real world, and in the real world we need evidence. Evidence gets you warrants. Evidence gets you arrests. Evidence gets you prosecutions and you've got absolutely none!"

"Don't talk to me about the real world! I'm out there in the real world doing proper police work. You just sit in here all day working on spreadsheets!"

And with that, he stormed out of the room, down the stairs and out of New Scotland Yard.

* * *

Painter walked along the embankment, retraced his steps, walked past Big Ben and Westminster Abbey and continued walking until he reached Westminster Cathedral. The passage of time, aided by the remarkable byzantine revival architecture brought him back to his senses. He gazed at the cool Portland stone and warm red brick construction, marvelling at how such different building materials could complement each other perfectly. If Painter was represented by the warm red brick, could he work with the cool, hard white stone of Veronica? It would need some kind of cement to bond them together. Several hours after he had stormed out of her office, the architecture helped him calm down and provided a metaphor for what he needed to do. He'd requested the meeting in the first place because he needed her permission to obtain the warrants. Without those his case and perhaps his entire career, were at a dead-end.

∞

Friday 30 October 2020

As soon as Painter woke up, he knew exactly what he had to do. Without his usual enthusiasm, he ate his breakfast, swallowed his blood pressure capsule, pecked Betty on the cheek absent-mindedly and set off for work. Avoiding his junior staff, he climbed up the stairs hoping the PA was prepared to talk to him, even if Veronica wouldn't. To his surprise, he was given an appointment for that afternoon, so busied himself with routine tasks while waiting to eat humble pie.

As the hour approached, he could feel his heart pumping even though he was sitting still at his desk. The organ pounded harder and harder against his ribs as he climbed the stairs and didn't slow down when the PA asked him to take a seat. She kept him waiting there for nearly 15 minutes before indicating that he could now enter the hallowed office. The degree certificate, resplendent in its gilt frame, looked down on him as if putting him in his place in the pecking order. He turned right to find Veronica sitting, stony faced, behind her desk. She didn't give a word of welcome, so Painter began the speech he'd rehearsed many times already:

"I've come to apologise for yesterday, ma'am. I was out of order and shouldn't have lost my cool, but I'm putting all my efforts into these murder cases and overreacted when you pointed out that I've no hard evidence so far."

When the speech came to an end, Veronica didn't say anything, but continued to stare at him. Eventually, she put him out of his misery:

"Your behaviour yesterday was unacceptable. I could have you disciplined for insubordination. I did wonder if you'd be better suited to working in the Met's traffic division than leading an important criminal investigation."

Painter swallowed hard, wondering what was to come next.

"However, I also reflected that my words were, perhaps, a little harsh, given the complexity of the murders you're investigating and the fact that you might now have a tenuous connection between the cases. I'll also acknowledge that you've a good track record in murder cases, even if your approaches can be unconventional. I therefore suggest we forget about yesterday, as long as there's no recurrence you understand, and discuss together in a proper professional way what progress you've made with these investigations."

"Thank you, ma'am. I feel we've made real progress and have brought some sense and order into a series of confusing murders. I can see the beginnings of a case coming together but agree we've no hard evidence yet."

"I can agree with that summary; what's your next step?"

"I don't know where the poison was brewed up but want to start by getting forensics from the kitchens of the 4 suspects because finding traces of ricin would provide our first real, solid fact. To do that, I'd need search warrants."

"I'll agree to that next step provided the magistrate you go to see is Mrs Hall. She and I attended a recent meeting of *Women in Justice* where she told me about a development with search warrants that she's pioneering. She specifically asked for you because I recollect that she's your old sparring partner."

"It's true, ma'am that Mrs Hall and I have come across each other from time to time. Her remit is to protect members of the public from excessive intrusion, whereas mine is to see if they can be excluded from my investigations. Often, the easiest way to achieve this is to issue a search warrant to rapidly get factual information about them. Where a police officer like myself can draw upon his experience to suggest that a crime may have been committed, I believe it's appropriate to request one. Mrs Hall and I have different views on when investigation should be permitted, but that difference is an essential and healthy feature of our system."

"Nice speech. Give it again when you see her."

* * *

Painter resented the fact that Veronica had sent him cap in hand to bow and scrape before Mrs Hall. He wondered what these two women had said about him while at their *Women in Justice* meeting. He imagined them describing him as an old-fashioned fuddy-duddy male without acknowledging that his methods got results. Was it fair that the Met's push to recruit more female staff meant that they now had informal ways of communicating between themselves and supporting each other? Was the Met now creating other back channels as potentially disruptive as the Masons had been for male officers in the past?

Despite these concerns, he did need her approval, so was pleased to find that Mrs Hall could see him that day. Promising himself to be on his best behaviour and to remain diplomatic throughout, he set off for what he knew wouldn't be an easy meeting.

"Inspector Painter. You and I have discussed this subject on several occasions. I have explained to you that I can only sign a search warrant if the public interest benefit exceeds the invasion of privacy for the citizen concerned. I have to base this decision on the evidence you present of a potential crime, but I can't see any evidence at all in your current case. Have I missed something?"

"No ma'am. You're correct in saying that we've no hard evidence yet. However, the circumstances are so unusual that I, as an experienced detective, believe that multiple murders may have been committed by a group of people.

Given the seriousness of these crimes, I'm requesting a warrant to search 4 houses, particularly the kitchens, to see if detection of residual traces of ricin poison provides the evidence that both you and I would like to see. If this request is denied, I fear that a perpetrator will attempt to destroy this evidence by cleaning and recleaning their flats once they find out that we're on to them."

Mrs Hall thought for a moment before giving Painter his answer:

"Your submission is weak. The only apparent link between these people is that they lived in the same street and attended the same primary school a quarter of a century ago and have recently returned to attend multiple funerals of their relatives during this dreadful pandemic. On the face of it, that doesn't seem like evidence to convince me that we're dealing with criminals. However, I agree the crimes are serious, you have circumstantial links to these people that could form a narrative of causality and there's a significant risk that crucial evidence may be tampered with. To address exactly these circumstances, I've pioneered a new conditional search warrant that becomes enforceable only if the person denies you permission to search their property when asked informally. The aim is to improve relations between the police and the public you serve. Many people who complain to us about police behaviour say you're too heavy handed when you burst into their homes. They say that they would have readily accepted intrusion into their lives if only they'd been asked politely. I'm willing to issue 4 of these new, somewhat experimental, conditional warrants if you agree to abide by their spirit and only use them where an individual refuses to cooperate. Are you willing to proceed on this basis and return to give me feedback about how they worked?"

Painter gritted his teeth as he gave the only answer possible under the circumstances:

"Yes, ma'am."

* * *

Painter needed a generous glass of malt and some rousing saxophone from Dexter Gordon as he plotted what the next working day held for the investigation.

Monday 2 November 2020

"Good morning, everyone. This is going to be a key day in our investigation. To get everyone on the same page, let me tell you again what I think happened. The Fatal Five were shocked when senior members of their extended families were taken away by Covid. They felt a strong sense of unfairness because these people all had customer facing jobs and were keeping the country going throughout the pandemic. I imagine the Fatal Five slipped away after each funeral to talk this through together at the cemetery. Resentment gradually built up and came to a head when one of the Five also succumbed to Covid. Yes, they snapped when Evie died and decided then to avenge her and the other victims. They made a list of the privileged people they had close access to and justified to themselves why they should get rid of each of them."

He paused for a second before continuing:

"Do a search on social media and newspapers to see if any of our 4 victims had said anything provocative about workers dying from Covid. I'm thinking of Norman Lamont's famous statement: **Rising unemployment and the recession have been the price that we have had to pay to get inflation down. That price is well worth paying.** Irrespective of such a possible stimulus, the now Fatal Four decided to target the only people they had access to. It must have looked heaven-sent to them that one owned the care home where Albert Harris senior died after contracting the infection, one owned the pub where Evie Potter worked and was exposed to infectious people, one ran London Transport whose bus was probably where Peter Johnson got infected and the fourth owned the supermarket where Margaret Jones acquired her dose of this new virus. They planned it carefully with poisoning of food the common means of access. Probably one of them made the ricin poison in their own kitchen. I'd put money on it being the caterer, but we'll keep an open mind and treat all 4 of them the same. My understanding is that they'd need a cooker hob and that residue will still be present in the extract fan even if they've given the kitchen a good clean. I want us to visit all 4 kitchens on the same evening with a forensic team and get samples. For Albert, we have the possibility that he did his cooking in Somerset, so get the police down there ready to do a sweep as soon as we say go. I want to choose a date when Lady Pilkington's staying in Regent's Park so will email her to request an interview. I won't tell her about taking samples until we're face to face."

"Do you want one of us to stay at each place to stop them warning any of the others?"

"No, Pippa; but I want their phone records so if one of them panics we'll have evidence of a conspiracy to show in court. They haven't called each other yet because I suspect they put all their plans together face to face when they were huddled in a group after each of the funerals in Nunhead."

Painter then told them about the conditional nature of the search warrants before giving another tutorial on the travelling salesman problem.

"We'll start at the furthest place in Neasden. We'll then take the Jubilee line to Baker Street. After a short walk to Regent's Park, we'll go on the Circle line to Barbican. We'll then go back on the Circle to Kings Cross and take the Victoria line to Highbury and Islington. Give all 4 addresses to the forensic people and have their vans waiting for us."

It was 6 PM when Painter looked at the scruffy door of the flat in Neasden and was admitted by Kevin Jones. To Painter's surprise, the man readily agreed to let forensic samples be taken. Painter waved in the team and left them to do their work because the flat was too small for everyone to be present. At Regent's Park, Lady Pilkington offered him sherry, which he politely declined, and agreed for samples to be taken. At the Barbican, Painter got lost among the rows of identical flats clad in brown tiles before locating the correct place and finding that Mandy Mitchell was willing for samples to be taken. Again, Louise Johnson raised no objection to the team collecting samples from her small flat in Islington.

Painter invited his junior officers to join him at 1 PM tomorrow, then returned home to his den, poured a large glass of malt and came to two conclusions. First, much to his surprise, the conditional warrants pioneered by Mrs Hall were a good idea because he hadn't had to produce them, yet they'd given him the power to insist on sampling if that proved necessary. Second, the 4 people, his only suspects, were not behaving like criminals trying to cover up their activities.

Painter refreshed his glass and looked at his CD collection to find some music that would match his mood. If all the forensic results turned out to be negative, he would be disappointed, so the wonderfully melancholic cover recording by Diana Ross of Billie Holliday's *Lady Sings the Blues* would fit the bill perfectly.

He let the sad, doleful tune play through to the end before stopping the CD. Painter was never one to dwell for too long on setbacks during a case so chose another female artist with a more uplifting tempo; *The Girl from Ipanema* by Astrid Gilberto. He hummed along to the tune until the finale and then let the rest of the CD play the other tunes by Stan Getz as his brain set to work.

His psyche was now ready to focus on the next step that would be necessary for the investigation. After refilling his glass with malt, he made his decision about how to move the case forward without demoralising his junior staff.

Tuesday 3 November 2020

Nick, Pippa and Baako were crammed into Painter's office waiting for the phone to ring. At exactly 13:00 Painter accepted the call and put his iPhone on speaker:

"I'm afraid that all samples from all 5 kitchens gave completely negative results. The positive control gave a good signal, showing that the assay worked, so we have to conclude that either these places were not used to make ricin, or they were cleaned up very carefully afterwards."

Painter thanked the scientist and ended the call.

"You don't seem too surprised, sir."

"You're right, Pippa. In my experience, criminals are always unhappy when we arrive to collect forensic samples. They ask to see a search warrant and dream up reasons why we should come back later, rather than do the tests now. None of our suspects acted that way, suggesting that they weren't afraid of us finding anything that could incriminate them."

"Where does that leave us now, sir?"

"It's possible that my image of these people conspiring to poison and kill multiple victims is wrong. However, that would mean we have multiple coincidences of 4 suspects attending the same primary school and each losing a close relative who happened to be employed by the boss they worked for. I'm not prepared to ignore these links, which are the only pieces of information that bring a coherent picture into the 4 deaths that are obviously connected. I propose therefore that we sampled the wrong sites. One or more of these people cooked up this poison but didn't use their own kitchens. I doubt if they borrowed the facilities at the houses of their parents or family because of the risk of poisoning their loved ones. Instead, I think they must have rented somewhere for a few days. The place must have a kitchen and would preferably be isolated away from prying eyes. Your job now is to go through the credit card statements of our 4 suspects to see if they made a booking for a place that fits that description. As to timing, they must have done it before the first poisoning and I doubt if any of this occurred to them before the first of their loved ones died; that's Albert Harris senior. Check all credit card entries between those dates and contact any companies, booking agents or estate agents to find out about any property that was rented. If a booking was made, I want that kitchen examined minutely."

∞

Thursday 5 November 2020

"There's one booking on Airbnb, sir. I checked with the company and it's a holiday let in Sussex rented between Saturday 8th and Saturday 15th August."

"Excellent. Was the booking made by the caterer?"

"Yes, sir; Mandy Mitchell."

"I thought so; she'd be the obvious one of the group to volunteer to cook up the ricin."

They showed him all the details and Painter gave his instructions.

"I've no jurisdiction down there, so liaise with Sussex Police to see when they can meet me on site with a forensic team and make sure that date's also convenient with the property owner who'll not want it booked by visitors when we appear talking about poisonings."

"Will do, sir. You also asked us to do a social media and newspaper trawl to look for anything provocative the 4 victims said about workers dying from Covid. Well, we've all done a lot of searching and the main points are as follows. Case 1, Sir John Pilkington, wasn't on social media, but he did give an interview for the *Financial Times*. They asked him lots of questions about the sectors his fund was invested in. When they got to care homes, they asked about the risk of Covid transmission and the exact words of his reply were: **the staff are used to deal-**

ing with infections. This could be interpretated as being dismissive of the risks his staff were exposed to. I don't know if any of the Fatal Five read the article but a link to it was included in a staff email and Albert Harris junior is on the mailing list. Case 2, Lord Yeast, also wasn't on social media. However, he pushed for the City of London to stay open during the pandemic and was quoted on this in the *Evening Standard* where he emphasised the importance of maintaining the local economy without mentioning the risks to staff. Like with Case 1, a link to the article was circulated to all staff, including Evie Potter, the sister of Mandy Mitchell. Case 3, William Randall, also wasn't on social media. But on the website of the TSSA, that's the Transport Salaried Staffs' Association, there's an open discussion where he, as CEO, argued against having screens on buses, citing the cost and disruption if vehicles had to be taken out of service to have them fitted. I don't know if Louise Johnson read it, but she's a paid-up member of the TSSA. Case 4, Günter Müller, was on lots of social media. On Twitter, he often emphasised his company's objective of keeping the cost of food down for ordinary people. He later acknowledged that his stores don't have the sort of facilities at checkout that full-service supermarkets provide. This was focussed on space for packing bags with purchases but implies lack of social distancing. Kevin Jones is on Twitter, but his mother Margaret wasn't."

"Thanks, Nick, for that useful background; I'll think about whether we can turn any of it into evidence that would stand up in court."

The rest of the meeting in Painter's office was brief, because, as he put it, he was off to the seaside.

The Circle line took him West to Victoria station where he caught an express train to Brighton taking just over an hour. Following the instructions provided, he walked out of the concourse to wait for the number 14 bus. It arrived after only 3 minutes and disgorged many people who sped off into the station. Hoping that the upper deck would now be empty, Painter climbed the curved staircase and grinned when he saw that the front seats were vacant. Dashing forward like a schoolboy, he claimed the two on the right-hand side, looking over his shoulder to dare anyone to ask him to share.

The bus started its journey by swaying through the one-way streets of Brighton. It headed East down North Street and then turned South to bring the Palace Pier directly into view. Painter watched as teenagers and families anticipating a day of frivolity and fun headed onto this structure. The bus turned left and began a long journey eastwards along the sea front with blocks of Regency apartments on his left, mostly painted in the signature primrose yellow, with some decorated in brilliant white. The journey was slow because cars kept turning in or pulling out from side roads off to the left. After 10 more minutes the traffic thinned out, the bus sped up and started to climb. Painter could now see the marina on the right-hand side followed by the cream-coloured stone of Roedean girls' school on the left. It looked impressive in the sunshine but would resemble Colditz Castle in the rain or the dark days of winter. Painter was glad that he and Betty had not had the financial resources to send their two daughters there.

The bus approached a roundabout where a different building dominated the skyline, promising wonderful sea views from every window. Painter was surprised to read a sign declaring it provided accommodation for those left visually impaired after fighting for our country. He hoped they benefitted from the fresh air even if they couldn't fully appreciate the view. Soon after, the bus slowed down for someone who had made a request to stop at the windmill; indeed, there was a wooden windmill painted black off to his left, standing high on a hill. The bus stopped again at the quaint, ancient village of Rottingdean; passengers got on but only two ventured upstairs and neither challenged his possession of the view from the front. The bus climbed and then descended more chalk hills with the bright, white edges clearly visible where they met the sea. He consulted his notes and prepared to push the request stop button when the name came up on the scrolling display. They entered the town of Peacehaven and soon Painter signalled his desire to get off. He thanked the driver and crossed the road where he saw Greggs the baker, exactly as instructed in his briefing notes. He walked to the end of the road to find that a wire fence was the only thing stopping him plunging over 100 feet to the base of the chalk cliff.

He had plenty of time before his appointment so walked along the cliff and into the town. He discovered a monument declaring that it marked the prime meridian so lay exactly due South of Greenwich. He walked back to the cliff edge, found the property that was listed on Airbnb and waited for his liaison from Sussex Police.

He was staring out to sea watching the ferry leaving Newhaven to make its cross-channel journey to Dieppe when his iPhone rang.

"Inspector Painter? It's Inspector Muriel Traynor here. I'm walking up the street and should reach the property within two minutes."

A woman, aged about 35, wearing a blue tailored suit with padded shoulders approached him and offered an outstretched hand.

"Welcome to Sussex. I hope we'll be able to assist you. The woman who owns this bungalow should be here shortly."

Painter used the time to brief her on his investigation and the need to get forensic samples from the whole house but particularly the kitchen.

"I've booked the team to arrive at half past so we

should soon get your samples and let you get back to London."

The owner of the property arrived and opened up. Painter was explaining that they needed to collect swabs from the property just as the forensic team arrived to do just that. He explained his requirements to them and then turned back to the owner. She was aged about 50, was carrying a clipboard, had short, dark hair and wore glasses with bright blue, plastic frames.

"How long have you owned this place?"

"I was born here. My husband and I bought a similar bungalow just 10 doors away about 25 years ago. It made it easier to keep an eye on my parents as they slowly got old. My dad died about 8 years ago. When my mum followed him 5 years ago, she left me the bungalow in her will. The view over the sea is better than the one from our place but makes it easier to rent out, so we stayed put. I started with a local estate agent, but they took 20% of the income so I moved it about 3 years ago to Airbnb."

"Who changes the sheets and cleans up at the end of a rental?"

"I do all of that. It's a time commitment and quite a bit of work but means I keep nearly all of the rental income."

"Did you keep a record of how well the place was looked after between the dates of Saturday 8 to Saturday 15 August that we sent you?"

"Yes, I have the checklist here. I keep one for every booking and use it to decide if I need to hold back some of the deposit they've paid. I take photos of the mess to support my decision to withhold some or all of the deposit. You've no idea, Inspector, what state some people leave the place in."

"How was it left when Mandy Mitchell checked out?"

"Here's my sheet; it was perfect. I did give it a going over with the vacuum but I needn't have bothered; the whole place was spotless."

"Did she stay here alone?"

"I don't know, Inspector, because I never met her. We email a door code to the person who makes the booking and they let themselves in and out."

"Are all of your bookings for a whole week?"

"We get plenty of bookings for one week during the summer, or even two weeks, but this time of year, most of them are weekends for DFLs."

"What does that mean?"

"That's down from London, Inspector. It's a common term used in Sussex," said Muriel Traynor.

"How do guests get rid of their domestic waste?"

"They put it in plastic bags and place it in the green or black wheelie bins outside."

"Green is for recycling, I suppose?"

"You'd think so, but black is for recycling and green is for anything else."

"What day are the bins collected by Brighton Council?"

"The green one is collected every Wednesday; the black one is taken every other Wednesday, but we're just over the border here for Lewes council, Inspector, so it's not Brighton's responsibility."

"That means that Mandy Mitchell's booking included a collection of her stuff on one Wednesday plus her stuff and that belonging to your next guest on the following Wednesday."

Muriel looked at her records.

"I always check the bins to make sure they're not overflowing. I didn't make any adverse notes about this booking so assume it was all tidy. There was no-one here in the week that followed."

"Do you ever look to see what's been put inside the plastic bags?"

"No, Inspector; I just make sure they're neat and tidy. If there were any loose glass bottles in the green bin, I'd move them to the black bin but I don't open plastic bags to make sure people have recycled properly."

Painter glanced out of the window and was surprised to see a rabbit hopping by. The two women smiled and told him he'd see plenty of rabbits here.

"Are they tame?"

"Not tame, but not very afraid of humans. Mind you,

if there's a dog nearby, you'll not see any rabbits for love nor money."

"Can you catch them?"

"Some people do, to keep as pets for the children. A neighbour 4 doors down has a hutch in her garden if you're interested."

Inspector Traynor escorted him to the bungalow where the woman explained that she simply left lettuce leaves out in the garden and the rabbits set up home there.

"We lock them away at night in that wooden cage to stop the fox getting them."

Painter thanked everyone for their assistance and set off to get the number 14 back to Brighton station. The seat at the very front of the bus was taken but he had an excellent view of the sea from a window seat on the left-hand side. The ever-changing view encouraged him to formulate a version of events that was supported during the train journey when he consulted his notebook to see what the Professor had told him.

Friday 6 November 2020

"Did you enjoy your day at the seaside, sir?"

"Yes, thanks," replied Painter; "it was very informative."

He told them about his trip and what he'd learned, culminating in his assessment:

"I think Mandy Mitchell made one or more batches of ricin in that bungalow. We'll hear later today if she left any traces. I think she also tested the potency by catching a rabbit and feeding it some of her concoction. Professor McDermott told me ages ago that ricin could be tested on mice and I emailed him today to confirm that rabbits would do just as well. I think she then put the rabbit carcass in a plastic bag and let Lewes council take it away. I suspect she planned this as an integral part of the process. She may have been to Sussex before and seen the rabbits or may have learned about them while researching her trip on Google. I can't prove this, of course, but it seems likely. As an alternative, is there any purchase on her credit card from a pet shop that might represent mice?"

"Nothing from a pet shop, sir, although there are several purchases from Greggs the bakers that week."

"Again, that's what I'd expect. She's a trained chef but chooses not to eat in the bungalow she's rented because she's afraid of getting poisoned. She'd have cleared up well - the owner said the place was spotless- but still didn't want to take the risk."

"When will we get the results of the tests, sir?"

"They're promised for 1300 today, so come back to this office just before then."

* * *

The group sat quietly around Painter's desk waiting for the phone to ring and all leant forward once he accepted the incoming call and selected speakerphone.

"We've lots of negative results for you again Inspector Painter, plus a few positives this time. All the positive results came from the grille of the extractor fan above the hob. However much people try to clean them there's often material stuck in the metal latticework."

Painter thanked the scientist, ended the call and they all celebrated the news.

"We've got her, sir," said Pippa.

"This is just what we needed," added Nick.

Painter noted that Baako was silent, so asked her for a comment.

"It's very good news, of course, but is it enough? I would expect a lawyer for the defence to argue that you have evidence of ricin poison at a particular address but no evidence of when it appeared or any evidence that

Mandy Mitchell put it there. The fact that she happened to rent the property may be entirely coincidental."

The group was quiet for a moment before Painter spoke:

"You're right, Baako and your training as a lawyer gives us good insight into what the CPS might conclude. However, finding the ricin now gives me a justification to bring Mandy Mitchell in for questioning. If she confesses, we've won. If not, we'll need to keep digging for more evidence while hoping that one of the other members of the Fatal Four cracks to give a confession."

* * *

Painter was pleased that he'd managed to get a time slot from the PA so began his climb upstairs to brief Veronica. He decided to be magnanimous in victory by acknowledging that her previous advice had worked out.

"Sit down, Bill; I gather congratulations are in order."

"Yes ma'am; although I want to start by saying that putting me on to Mrs Hall the magistrate was very helpful. I wasn't convinced by her conditional warrants at first but, now I've seen them in action, I'm a convert. All 4 suspects readily let us into their houses, so I didn't need to produce the warrants. Their behaviour told me they'd nothing to fear from the forensics. I therefore looked for an alternative, found that one of them had booked a remote bungalow for a week through Airbnb and that led us to the crime scene. It's the first time that we've found ricin outside the bodies of the 4 victims."

"Well done for that nice bit of detective work. What's next?"

"I'm sure that these 4 suspects conspired to murder our 4 victims, but now need evidence to prove it. I'd like to bring in Mandy Mitchell, the caterer who hired the bungalow, for questioning under caution. If she confesses, we can wrap up all 4 cases quickly. If she doesn't, I'd like to put pressure on the other 3 co-conspirators by bringing them in one by one to also be interviewed under caution. My hope is that one of them will spill the beans."

Once he'd realised his inadvertent pun, Painter suppressed a laugh and escaped from the intimidating office, confident that Veronica would not have seen the funny side of this case.

* * *

"We now come to a critical phase in our investigation. We think we know who killed these 4 people and why they did it. Motivation and opportunity are thus fairly well established, but we need to work on the means. We need to get from them exactly what food item they contaminated on each occasion and how they persuaded the victims to consume it. This, coupled with a confession, would produce a compelling case to take to court. However, we need to anticipate that each suspect will not help us by confessing. We need to build a case against them by showing how much we know and implying that we can prove it. To do this, we'll interview them one at a time under caution, taping their answers as we go along. I find it helps to ask suspects some questions we already know the answer to as a way of getting them used to telling the truth. We can then observe any changes in their demeanour when they have to lie in response to another question. This will be good for your training, Pippa, so I want you to help me draw up the list of standard questions and join me in conducting the interviews. Nick and Baako can watch through the two-way mirror and note down any points they think need to be followed up. We'll start with Mandy Mitchell, the caterer we suspect of brewing up the ricin."

Monday 9 November 2020

It was still dark as Pippa and Painter met up at New Scotland Yard for a 6 AM dawn raid.

"This is one of the few times I use a squad car. It's useful to have an officer in uniform in case the suspect is uncooperative and it would be difficult to escort them through the underground system where they could escape. I imagine you're used to using squad cars to bring people in for questioning."

"Yes, sir. We had no public transport to speak of in Devon and Cornwall, so everything was done by car."

At the Barbican, Painter retraced his steps along rows of near identical flats with brown, glazed tiles before locating the correct place. After ringing the bell repeatedly, Mandy Mitchell came on the answerphone and reluctantly let them in.

"I apologise for disturbing you at this hour Miss but require you to come to New Scotland Yard to be interviewed under caution."

"What's this all about, Inspector?"

"That will become clear as we go along Miss, but we believe you have information about the death by poisoning of Lord Yeast."

"This is very inconvenient. What if I refuse to come with you?"

"Then I'll have to arrest you on suspicion of murder."

Mandy turned pale on hearing this.

"I believe I'm entitled to be represented by a solicitor."

"Indeed you are and I would recommend that you contact him or her now. If you don't have a solicitor, we'll appoint one for you."

"I'll telephone now. I also need to let my colleague know that I'll be late for work. You'll presumably also let me dress?"

"Yes, Miss. Sergeant Pippa Trelawny will stay with you while you get ready."

After 20 minutes, Mandy came back into the living area wearing a pale blue suit with padded shoulders.

"There's no-one at my solicitor's office at this hour but I've left a message on her voice mail and sent an email asking her to contact me urgently. Obviously, I'll not be answering any questions until she arrives."

Back at New Scotland Yard, they settled her into interview room 4 and gave her a cup of coffee. It was 10:30 before the solicitor arrived. She had a private discussion with her client before the interview started.

"For the benefit of the tape, the people present are Inspector Bill Painter, Sergeant Pippa Trelawny, Miss Mandy Mitchell and Miss Olivia Wright, her solicitor. I have explained that Miss Mitchell will be interviewed under caution and that her replies may be presented in court. Let me start by asking if it's correct to say that you were born in Nunhead, lived at 180 Ivydale Road and went to Ivydale School, Nunhead?"

"That is correct."

"Did you go to church at St Silas?"

"Yes, I did."

"Could the sermons be described as advocating an eye for an eye?"

Mandy whispered to the solicitor who replied:

"My client declines to answer questions of a personal nature."

"Were you friends with Albert Harris, Louise Johnson and Kevin Jones?"

"My client declines to answer questions of a personal nature."

"Did the four of you, plus your sister Evie, hang out together in a group?"

Mandy nodded to the solicitor who replied:

"My client declines to answer questions of a personal nature."

"Did you meet up regularly in the garden that backs onto the cemetery?"

"My client declines to answer questions of a personal nature."

"Let's move on to your later life. You attended St Saviours Girls Church of England School in Southwark, where you passed A level Economics and English."

"That is correct."

"You then worked in a restaurant in the Old Kent Road for 3 years."

"That is correct."

"You then moved to a different restaurant in Barts Square EC1."

"That is correct."

"After 3 more years, you established your own business supplying catering services to the City of London."

"That is correct."

"You're single and live in the Barbican."

"I live in the Barbican, but my marital status is no business of yours."

"Let's now turn to the fateful day when Lord Yeast died. I believe you served him food and drink as part of a tasting session?"

Mandy whispered in the ear of her solicitor before replying:

"Yes, my company was contracted to produce food for assessment. I placed the food in front of Lord Yeast and the other 5 or 6 people seated around the table. The food was prepared in the kitchen of my company and transported to the City. The drinks were prepared by the brewing company, not me. Let me state for the record that identical food was given to all people around the table. I understand that no-one else in the group was taken ill."

"I can confirm that, Miss."

Painter paused before asking his next question:

"Lord Yeast died from eating a poison called ricin. Did you contaminate the food intended for Lord Yeast with ricin or any other poison?"

"No, I did not. I would also point out that one of your officers telephoned me on the day after Lord Yeast's tragic death and arranged for the leftover food to be examined. I understand that no poison was detected in this."

"I can confirm that as well, Miss."

"Then I fail to see why you're trying to blame me for his death."

"Let's move on to some other questions. Have you ever been to Peacehaven in East Sussex?"

"Yes, I have."

"I understand you made a booking through Airbnb to stay in a bungalow there for a week between Saturday 8th and Saturday 15th August."

"That is correct."

"Did you stay there alone?"

"That's a personal question, Inspector, which I'll advise my client not to answer."

"Are you familiar with rabbits?"

Mandy looked surprised, glanced towards her solicitor who quickly replied:

"Again, that's a question intruding into the personal life of my client that I'll advise her not to answer."

Painter, also surprised, looked towards Pippa, noticed

a smirk on her face and realised he'd gone down the wrong pathway.

"Let me clarify. I wish to know if you are familiar with the rodents kept as pets known as rabbits or bunnies, perhaps."

"No comment."

"What was the purpose of your visit to Peacehaven?"

"My client went there for rest and recreation."

"Then let me tell you that forensic samples from the property revealed traces of ricin; exactly the same poison that killed Lord Yeast."

Painter paused before asking his next question:

"Did you make a batch of ricin poison while you were staying at Peacehaven?"

Instantly receiving **no comment** from both of them, Painter continued:

"Let me turn now to a different set of questions. I believe you attended the 4 funerals of people close to you who died from Covid. Did you attend the funeral of Albert Harris on Tuesday 19 May 2020?"

"Yes, I did."

"Did you attend the funeral of Margaret Jones on Thursday 28 May 2020?"

"Yes, I did."

"Did you attend the funeral of Peter Johnson on Thursday 18 June?"

"Yes, I did."

"Did you attend the funeral of your sister, Evie Potter on Monday 22 June?"

"Yes, I did."

Painter noticed that Mandy's lip had quivered as she answered the last question.

"I apologise if it's difficult for you to talk about your sister, but I understand that Evie was only 33 years old and had serious medical problems that put her at risk of dying from Covid."

"That is correct."

"She worked as a barmaid in a pub in Peckham didn't she?"

"Yes, she did."

"Do you think that's where she contracted the virus that gave her Covid?"

"No comment."

"Do you blame the brewery that employed her?"

"No comment."

"Did you seek retribution from the head of that brewery, Lord Yeast?"

"No comment."

"Just one last question. You gave us the details of your mobile phone when we first interviewed you. Do you have access to a second phone, a pay as you go perhaps?"

"My client declines to answer any questions of a personal nature, including that last one. Inspector Painter: in the past half hour, you've put many questions to my client and made a series of serious accusations. You apparently have evidence of ricin poison at a particular address in Sussex. My client acknowledges staying at the same address, but you have no evidence that she produced the poison there, as you allege. For the tape, my client wishes to state that she's innocent of these accusations and resents them. Please contact me, not her, if you wish to put any more questions to her in the future. We are now leaving New Scotland Yard unless you propose to arrest my client."

Painter joined the others who had been following the proceedings through the two-way mirror.

"What do you think, Nick?"

"Well, she clearly won't be rolling over and confessing today. In fact, she's going to make our lives as difficult as possible. I suppose we could dig deeper into the questions she gave a no comment answer to."

"What about you, Baako?"

"I'll need to go back over the tape carefully, but my impression was that she answered questions of a factual nature, which she realised we could verify, but declined to answer anything else. I was also a bit confused about the rabbit question; what was that all about?"

"It's a matter of colloquial English that I'm going to let Pippa explain to you."

Tuesday 10 November 2020

Pippa had a lie in this time because Painter chose 7:30 AM for the dawn raid.

"I know Albert's not going anywhere because I telephoned Lady Pilkington yesterday and asked if her staff would be free for a follow up interview this morning."

At Regent's Park, Mrs Perkins eventually answered the persistent doorbell.

"I apologise for disturbing you at this hour, but I need to see Albert."

The chauffer was summoned and appeared, already dressed, but without his smart jacket.

"I require you to come to New Scotland Yard to be interviewed under caution."

"What for, Inspector?"

"That will become clear as we go along, but we suspect you've information about the death by poisoning of Sir John Pilkington."

"I'll telephone my solicitor and won't say a word until she's arrived."

At New Scotland Yard, Painter noted that the solicitor representing Albert Harris was none other than Olivia Wright.

"For the benefit of the tape, the people present are Inspector Bill Painter, Sergeant Pippa Trelawny, Albert

Harris and Miss Olivia Wright, his solicitor. I have explained that Mr Harris will be interviewed under caution and that his replies may be presented in court. Let me start by asking if it's correct to say that you were born in Nunhead, lived at 178 Ivydale Road and went to Ivydale School, Nunhead?"

"That's right."

"Did you go to church at St Silas?"

"Yes, I did."

"Could the sermons be described as advocating an eye for an eye?"

"My client declines to answer questions of a personal nature."

"Were you friends with Mandy Mitchell, Louise Johnson, Kevin Jones and Evie Mitchell?"

"My client declines to answer questions of a personal nature."

"Did the five of you hang out together in a group?"

"My client declines to answer questions of a personal nature."

"Did the 5 of you meet up regularly in the garden that backs onto the cemetery?"

"My client declines to answer questions of a personal nature."

"Let's move on to your later life. You went Ark Walworth Academy on the Old Kent Road and passed GCSEs."

"That's right."

"Your life has always involved cars. You worked in a local garage then started driving around London to get the knowledge needed to drive a black taxi."

"That's right."

"You then changed tack to obtain a private hire licence instead and completed a drivers' course through the British Chauffeurs Guild."

"That's right. I realised that GPS sat nav was changing things, so it wasn't worth studying for the knowledge."

"You then moved to work for a limousine hire company."

"That's right."

"You then replied to an advert placed by Sir John Pilkington and became his chauffeur."

"That's right."

"That post requires you to live alternately in Somerset and Regent's Park as your employer moves back and forth. Do you mind that disruption to life?"

"I'm very happy working for Sir John and Lady Pilkington. Moving around isn't a problem for me. I'm single and get to drive a Rolls Royce for a living."

"Let's now turn to the fateful day when Sir John died. I believe you drove him to Mayfair that morning?"

"That's right. I gave all the details about timings when I made my statement."

"Did you give any food or drink to Sir John during the journey?"

"No."

Painter paused and looked directly at Albert:

"Think carefully before you answer the next question because you are being interviewed under caution. If it turns out that you're not telling the truth, then you may be prosecuted. Because we're investigating the crime of murder, the charge would be one of murder that normally carries a long jail sentence."

Albert swallowed hard and looked straight at Painter.

"Sir John died from eating or drinking a poison called ricin. Are you sure that Sir John didn't eat or drink anything during the journey to Mayfair?"

"Yes, I am sure. I'll also point out that your officers tested the car and I understand that none of this poison was found there."

"That's correct."

"Then why do you keep asking me if I gave him any food or drink?"

"Let me turn now to a different set of questions. I believe you attended the 4 funerals of people close to you who died from Covid. Did you attend the funeral of Albert Harris on Tuesday 19 May 2020?"

"Yes, I did."

"He was your grandfather and you were named after him I believe."

"That's right."

"I understand he lived at number 178 Ivydale Road all his adult life and worked as a painter and decorator."

"That's right."

"As well as being a grandfather to you, was he a grandfather figure to all 5 children in the group?"

"My client declines to answer questions of a personal nature."

"Did you attend the funeral of Margaret Jones on Thursday 28 May 2020?"

"Yes, I did."

"Did you attend the funeral of Peter Johnson on Thursday 18 June 2020?"

"Yes, I did."

"Did you attend the funeral of Evie Potter on Monday 22 June 2020?"

"Yes, I did."

"That's 4 funerals to attend in a short time. Going back to the first one, do you blame the care home for letting your grandfather Albert contract the virus that gave him Covid?"

"No comment."

"Did you know that the care home where Albert Harris died is owned ultimately by Raffles Private Equity?"

"No comment."

"Do you blame Raffles Private Equity for your grandfather's death?"

"No comment."

"Did you seek retribution from the head of Raffles Private Equity, Sir John Pilkington?"

"No comment."

"Just two more questions before we finish. You gave us the details of your mobile phone when we first interviewed you. Do you have access to a second phone, a pay as you go perhaps?"

"My client declines to answer questions of a personal nature. What's your second question?"

"How long have you known Miss Olivia Wright and how did she come to be your solicitor?"

"My client declines to answer questions of a personal nature, including those covered by solicitor-client confidentiality. I must say, Inspector Painter that, once again, you've put many questions to my client and made a serious accusation. I appreciate that you have evidence of ricin poisoning, but my client has stated clearly that he has no knowledge about this. For the tape, my client states that he's innocent of the accusations you made and resents you putting them to him. Unless you are prepared to charge him, this interview is terminated."

Once they had left, Painter joined the others.

"What do you all think?"

"It's similar to Mandy's interview, sir. That solicitor's blocking all of the questions we don't already know the answers to."

"I agree, Nick. I now want you all to focus on two things. How are the 4 of them communicating, including with this solicitor? Have there been any recent contacts between their phones? If not, have they got additional phones we don't know anything about? Second, dig into the background of that solicitor. Baako, you've got legal skills, so search for all the cases she's recorded as being involved in. Check those against all of the names of the Famous Five to see when one of them first made contact with her. Also, look into her personal background; I'd be particularly interested to hear that she grew up in Nunhead."

* * *

Painter poured himself a generous glass of malt whisky and selected a CD to help him think through the problem. As the wonderful arrangements by Jacques Loussier of Bach's melodies flowed, his brain got to work.

Painter knew he would have to use his secret weapon. It was the basis of how he managed to crack difficult cases, but he used it only when really necessary. If it gave him a lead, he then had the difficulty of creating a back story to explain to his colleagues, as well as to any future barrister for the defence, how he'd come by the information legally. He drained his glass, turned down the volume on the CD player and dialled a number he hadn't used for a while:

"Hello Tommy; remember me?"

"'corse I does Mr Painter. What can I do for you this time?"

"If I'm in the same room as someone, can a gadget or app on my iPhone make a note of their telephone number, even if it's a non- registered pay as you go mobile?"

"Meet me at 9 tomorrow in that caf we know so well and I'll give you a few options."

∞

Wednesday 11 November 2020

Painter approached the greasy spoon thinking that the façade hadn't changed a bit over the years. Prompt as always, Tommy was already sitting in a quiet corner seat.

"Builder's tea with three sugars isn't it, Tommy?"

"You've got a good memory, Mr Painter."

"I have, Tommy. It seems like only yesterday that I decided not to throw the book at you but to find you a friendly probation officer to give you a second chance to get a legit career without a criminal record."

"I'm very grateful Mr Painter and would like to 'elp if I can. I'm all legit now, after followin' your advice but a business acquaintance of mine 'as a device that records the numbers of nearby phones. But you need to be standing near to the person when it 'appens; Bluetooth innit; sends data over short distances. I've brought you this burner phone with the device on it, 'cos I'm guessin' you don't wanna use your New Scotland Yard phone."

Thursday 12 November 2020

Pippa was up early because Painter chose 6:30 AM for the dawn raid in Islington.

Louise Johnson eventually answered the persistently ringing doorbell and Painter was immediately struck by how attractive she was, even without makeup. Standing before him was a tall and trim blonde with blue eyes, a generous bust, high cheekbones and a wide, soft mouth.

"I apologise for disturbing you at this hour, Miss but I require you to come to New Scotland Yard to be interviewed under caution."

"Whatever for, Inspector?"

"That will become clear as we progress through our questions, but we suspect you've information about the death by poisoning of William Randall."

"I'm not saying a word until I've spoken to my solicitor."

"That's good practice, Miss. Please leave a message asking her, or possibly him, to join us all at New Scotland Yard."

When the solicitor arrived, Painter was not surprised to be looking at Olivia Wright.

"For the benefit of the tape, the people present are Inspector Bill Painter, Sergeant Pippa Trelawny, Louise

Johnson and Miss Olivia Wright, her solicitor. I have explained that Miss Johnson will be interviewed under caution and that her replies may be presented in court. Let me start by asking if it's correct to say that you were born in Nunhead, lived at 184 Ivydale Road and went to Ivydale School, Nunhead?"

"Yes, that's correct."

"Did you go to church at St Silas?"

"Yes, I did."

"Could the sermons be described as advocating an eye for an eye?"

"My client declines to answer questions of a personal nature."

"Were you friends with Albert Harris, Mandy Mitchell, Kevin Jones and Evie Mitchell?"

"My client declines to answer questions of a personal nature."

"Did the 5 of you hang out together in a group?"

"My client declines to answer questions of a personal nature."

"Did the 5 of you meet up regularly in the garden that backs onto the cemetery?"

"My client declines to answer questions of a personal nature."

"Let's move on to your later life. You attended Kingsdale Foundation School in Dulwich where you passed A level English."

"Yes, that's correct."

"You then did a 6 months' secretarial course by distance learning through Keystone Courses."

"Yes, that's correct."

"You joined London Transport as a trainee secretary and have worked your way up through the organisation to become William Randall's secretary."

"Yes, that's correct."

"You rent the flat in Islington where we collected you this morning."

"Yes, that's correct."

"You're single and live there alone."

"My client declines to answer questions of a personal nature."

"Let's now turn to the fateful day when William Randall died. You told us in your statement that his normal practice was to take no food or drink at lunchtime."

"Yes, that's correct."

"Did you give any food or drink to him on that day?"

"Only the coffee that I made for him. As I said in my statement, this was drunk by other members of staff, including me."

Painter paused and looked directly at the beautiful woman in front of him:

"Think carefully before you answer my next question because you're being interviewed under caution. If it turns out that you're not telling the truth, then you may be prosecuted. Because we're investigating the crime of murder, the charge would be one of murder that normally carries a long jail sentence."

Louise looked straight at Painter but said nothing.

"William Randall died from eating or drinking a poison called ricin. Are you sure that he didn't eat or drink anything that day apart from the coffee you've already told us about?"

"Yes, I'm sure."

"Let me turn now to a different set of questions. I believe you attended the 4 funerals of people close to you who died from Covid. Did you attend the funeral of Albert Harris on Tuesday 19 May 2020?"

"Yes, I did."

"As well as being a grandfather to Albert, was he a grandfather figure to all 5 children in the group?"

"My client declines to answer questions of a personal nature."

"Did you attend the funeral of Margaret Jones on Thursday 28 May 2020?"

"Yes, I did."

"Did you attend the funeral of your father, Peter Johnson on Thursday 18 June 2020?"

"Yes, I did."

"He lived at number 184 Ivydale Road and worked all his life as a bus driver, I understand."

"Yes, that's correct."

"As well as being your biological father, was Peter Johnson a father figure to the whole group?"

"My client declines to answer questions of a personal nature."

"Did you attend the funeral of Evie Potter on Monday 22 June 2020?"

"Yes, I did."

"That's 4 funerals to attend in a matter of 5 short weeks. Going back to the funeral of your father, do you blame London Transport for letting him contract the virus that gave him Covid?"

"No comment."

"Did you seek retribution for your father's death from the head of London Transport, William Randall?"

"No comment."

"Were you having an affair with William Randall?"

"My client declines to answer questions of a personal nature."

"You gave us the details of your mobile phone when we first interviewed you. Do you have access to a second phone, a pay as you go perhaps?"

"My client declines to answer questions of a personal nature."

"How long have you known Miss Olivia Wright and how did she come to be your solicitor?"

"My client declines to answer questions of a personal

nature, including those covered by solicitor-client confidentiality."

"We've now come to the end of my questions for today, but it may be necessary to interview you again."

"Inspector Painter; once again, you've put many questions to my client and made some serious accusations. I appreciate that you have evidence of ricin poisoning, but my client has stated clearly that she has no knowledge about this. For the tape, my client states that she's innocent of the accusations you made and resents you putting them to her. Unless you're prepared to charge her, we will now leave New Scotland Yard. If you wish to interview her again, please contact my office, not my client."

Once they were gone, Painter joined the others.

"What do you all think?"

"It's similar to all the interviews, sir. That solicitor's blocking everything."

"I agree, Nick. Did your investigations find anything that could help us?"

"We checked again and there haven't been any contacts between their phones apart from each suspect calling Olivia Wright when we arrived at their home. I asked the tech people and there's no way of finding out if they have a burner phone unless we get a warrant and search them and their property."

"You asked me to look into the background of the solicitor, sir" said Baako. "I searched through all her recorded cases. I then checked these against all of the names of the Fatal Five and the only one that came up was Mandy Mitchell. It seems that Olivia Wright did the conveyancing when Mandy bought her flat in the Barbican. I also looked into her personal background and found she grew up in Guildford, which I understand is miles away from Nunhead."

"Another dead end for these cases; I was hoping that Ms Wright would turn out to be one of the Nunhead gang. Right, everyone; we've got to solve these cases, so keep digging."

* * *

The builder's tea with three sugars was waiting for Tommy who took the burner phone from Painter and gave his opinion.

"You 'ave a few numbers 'ere."

As he called them out quietly, Painter checked his iPhone.

"That's my Sergeant, that's my iPhone, that's the solicitor, that's the person I'm interested in, but I already know that number. Why didn't it capture any more?"

"The person might 'ave left their phone at home. They might 'ave switched it off. Is your person a bird?"

"Yes."

"Well, she might 'ave it in a different handbag; one

she takes just when she needs her special phone."

"Thanks for your help. I'll try again during the interview of the next person and I'm grateful to you for showing me what to do."

"It's been a pleasure 'elping you again Mr Painter; keep in touch."

∞

Friday 13 November 2020

Pippa was up early because Painter chose 6:30 AM for the dawn raid in Neasden.

Kevin Jones promptly opened the scruffy door of the flat in response to the persistently ringing doorbell.

"I apologise for disturbing you at this hour, Mr Jones but I require you to come to New Scotland Yard to be interviewed under caution."

"Why's that, Inspector?"

"We suspect you've information about the death by poisoning of Günter Müller."

"I'm not saying anything until I've phoned my solicitor."

"That's fine with us. Just leave a voice mail asking Olivia Wright to join us all at New Scotland Yard."

Kevin looked stunned as he turned away to make the call.

* * *

Painter's gut feeling that the solicitor would turn out to be Olivia Wright was proven correct when she arrived at New Scotland Yard later that morning.

"For the tape recording, the people present are Inspector Bill Painter, Sergeant Pippa Trelawny, Kevin

Jones and Miss Olivia Wright, his solicitor. I've explained that Mr Jones will be interviewed under caution and that his replies may be presented in court. Let me start by asking if it's correct to say that you were born in Nunhead, lived at 186 Ivydale Road and went to Ivydale School, Nunhead?"

"Correct."

"Did you go to church at St Silas?"

"Yes, I did."

"Could the sermons be described as advocating an eye for an eye?"

"My client declines to answer questions of a personal nature."

"Were you friends with Albert Harris, Mandy Mitchell, Louise Johnson and Evie Mitchell?"

"My client declines to answer questions of a personal nature."

"Did the 5 of you hang out together in a group?"

"My client declines to answer questions of a personal nature."

"Did the 5 of you meet up regularly in the garden that backs onto the cemetery?"

"My client declines to answer questions of a personal nature."

"Let's move on to your later life. You went to Harris Academy Peckham where you passed GCSEs."

"Correct."

"You then started work at your local Tesco store in Peckham."

"Correct."

"After 3 years you moved to Asda, also in Peckham."

"Correct."

"After 4 more years, you went to Sainsburys, still in Peckham, where I understand you got used to the computer systems they use."

"Correct."

"Then, last year, you used your computer experience to get a promotion and move to this new German supermarket in Neasden as a senior packer."

"Correct."

"That means you've lived in Peckham all your life until you got this latest job when you moved into a rented flat in Neasden where we collected you this morning."

"Correct."

"You're single and live there alone."

"My client declines to answer questions of a personal nature."

"Let's now turn to the fateful day when Günter Müller died. You told us in your statement that you saw him walking through the building."

"Correct."

"Did you give any food or drink to him on that day?"

"No."

Painter paused and looked directly at the young man in front of him:

"Think carefully before you answer my next question because you're being interviewed under caution. If it turns out that you're not telling the truth, then you may be prosecuted. Because we're investigating the crime of murder, the charge would be one of murder that normally carries a long jail sentence."

Kevin fidgeted in his chair a little but continued to look straight at Painter without saying anything.

"Günter Müller died from eating or drinking a poison called ricin. Are you sure that you didn't give him anything to eat or drink that day?"

"Yes, I'm sure."

"For the avoidance of any doubt, did you give Mr Müller a sweet known as a gummy bear?"

"No, I didn't."

"Let me turn now to a different set of questions. I believe you attended the 4 funerals of people close to you who died from Covid. Did you attend the funeral of Albert Harris on Tuesday 19 May 2020?"

"Yes."

"As well as being a grandfather to Albert, was he a grandfather figure to all 5 children in the group?"

"My client declines to answer questions of a personal nature."

"Did you attend the funeral of your mother, Margaret Jones on Thursday 28 May 2020?"

Kevin swallowed hard before giving his trademark one word answer:

"Yes."

"She lived at number 186 Ivydale Road and worked at a supermarket checkout, I understand."

"Yes."

"As well as being your biological mother, was Margaret Jones a mother figure to the whole group?"

"My client declines to answer questions of a personal nature."

"Did you attend the funeral of Peter Johnson on Thursday 18 June 2020?"

"Yes, I did."

"Did you attend the funeral of Evie Potter on Monday 22 June 2020?"

"Yes, I did."

"That's 4 funerals to attend within barely 5 weeks. Going back to the funeral of your mother, do you blame this new German supermarket for letting her contract the virus that gave her Covid?"

"No comment."

"Did you seek retribution for your mother's death from the head of the supermarket, Günter Müller?"

"No comment."

"You gave us the details of your mobile phone when

we first interviewed you. Do you have access to a second phone, a pay as you go perhaps?"

"My client declines to answer questions of a personal nature."

"How long have you known Miss Olivia Wright and how did she come to be your solicitor?"

"My client declines to answer questions of a personal nature, including those covered by solicitor-client confidentiality."

"We've now come to the end of my questions for today, but it may be necessary to interview you again."

"Inspector Painter; once again, you've put many questions to my client and made a serious accusation. I appreciate that you have evidence of ricin poisoning, but my client has no knowledge about this. For the tape, my client states that he's innocent of the accusation you made and resents you putting it to him. Unless you're prepared to charge him, we will now leave New Scotland Yard. If you wish to interview him again please contact my office, not my client."

Once they were gone, Painter popped to the loo, locked the door of the cubicle, turned on the secret phone and looked at the screen. He knew that if someone discovered him doing this, he would be disciplined and potentially sacked.

He repeated the actions that Tommy had shown him. The screen showed numbers that he identified as belonging to the solicitor, Pippa, himself and the number provided by Kevin Jones, along with another number not listed in his iPhone. He turned off the burner phone and knew exactly what he'd do next. He joined the others and asked:

"What do you all think?"

"It's similar to all the interviews, sir. That solicitor's blocking everything."

"I agree, Nick. Because the solicitor's blocking progress in our investigation I think we need to pause and regroup. We'll take tomorrow as a rest day and return to the problem refreshed on Monday."

This time the conversation was different once the junior officers were out of earshot.

"You could have knocked me over with a feather. It's like he's had a personality change and finally realised that his juniors are humans who need a day off from time to time."

"In all the years I've worked for him I can't remember another example of him giving me a day off unless it was forced on him by circumstances. I'm pleasantly surprised by his generosity."

"Let's not waste any more time then. I'll go sightseeing in this famous city tomorrow."

Saturday 14 November 2020

Painter didn't tell Betty about the rest day for fear of being dragged off to a sofa shop. Instead, he sent the new number to Tommy and asked for advice.

Soon, the builder's tea with three sugars was waiting for Tommy.

"'ello Mr Painter. That number you sent me might be just what you wanted. Would you like to know it's a pay as you go phone as you expected? Would you also like to know where it was bought and when?"

"Yes please to both questions."

"In Peckham Rye at the EE shop on Thursday 28 May 2020."

Painter noted down the details.

"My colleague also worked 'is magic on the Internet and found what other phones that number's called. Would you be interested in knowin' that it's only called 4 other numbers and they're all consecutive?"

Painter paused for a moment to let the significance of this fact settle into his brain.

"That's brilliant, Tommy. That means all 5 phones were bought at the same time. This is very helpful information, so I'm indebted to you. I didn't know you could find that sort of information on the web."

"Neither did I Mr Painter; I dunno how my colleague does it."

* * *

The malt sloshed into the glass with a vigour that demonstrated Painter's determination to create a great plan of action. To accompany it he needed some equally great jazz and Miles Davis would fit the bill perfectly.

Painter's first objective was to catch these villains by providing the hard evidence the CPS and a court would require. His second objective was to avoid being caught himself. If the Met Professional Standards knocked on the door now, what would they find out? The worst that could happen is a criticism for meeting an old informant without declaring this to his superior beforehand. He was certain that Tommy wouldn't give anything away. However, there was another force of nature that might catch him out, a bright barrister for the defence. If he or she became suspicious of how Painter had identified the 5 burner phones s/he could interrogate him and his junior officers for any gaps in his version of events. To protect against this, he needed a watertight explanation. To think of one, he needed to change to another CD by the same artist and refresh the now empty glass.

Under the influence of the mellow music and the warming whisky he thought through his alternative version of reality ready to be made real immediately in the morning.

Monday 16 November 2020

"Good morning, everyone. I hope you enjoyed your rest day. It's back to work now and I've an interesting possibility for you all to follow up."

The 3 faces listening intently to his every word remained silent, so he continued:

"Our investigation is blocked so we need to change tack by chasing how they communicate. The great detective Sherlock Holmes used what's called abductive reasoning, aiming to provide the best explanation of a unique apparently mystifying event when he said: **when you have eliminated the impossible, whatever remains, however improbable, must be the truth.** My system of detective work builds upon this concept by asking: **if this is the answer what is the question?** We're going to apply that concept now to the answer that we believe, but don't yet have proof of, that these 4 suspects each have a burner phone and are using them to communicate with each other. If we take that assumption as gospel, we then have the question of how they came to get them. Pippa: suggest a time when they bought these phones."

"I suppose they could each have bought a phone many years ago."

"That's a possibility of course, but let's ignore it for now, because why would 4 separate people choose a pay as you go rather than a normal phone on a contract, especially when they already have a mobile? Nick, make another suggestion."

"They could have got together and decided they should each have a phone to communicate within the group. I recollect that, at present, they each use a phone provided by their workplace, so perhaps they wanted a way of discussing things of a private nature."

"These are good thoughts; we're making progress now. What do you suggest, Baako?"

"In my experience, gang members have phones to communicate with each other and get issued with them when they join up."

"Another good point. Let's follow that further; when did our suspects join the Fatal Five?"

"When they went to primary school, sir."

"That's right, Pippa, but I doubt if they bought burner phones then. Even if they did, they must be obsolete by now. We've also no evidence that the Fatal Five stayed together; for example, you couldn't find a single example of one telephoning or emailing another and they've no links on social media. No, I think the Fatal Five only regrouped when their relatives started dying from Covid; a bit like a rock band coming back for a reunion. So, when would they all meet up again?"

"At the first funeral," offered Nick.

"Correct and that's a real possibility. But I think it's

more likely to be after the second funeral. The first one would be a sad occasion, but Albert senior was elderly after all. I suspect that sadness was amplified at the second funeral and joined by the emotion of anger. Did they meet after the funeral, perhaps in the garden or even by pushing through the bushes into the cemetery where they used to meet as kids? If it felt fun, like old times, they could have agreed to resurrect the Fatal Five to avenge the deaths of close relatives. They may have been influenced by the fire and brimstone, eye for an eye, type of sermon that they sat through every Sunday."

"But who would they want to target at that stage? Remember that they wouldn't know about the third and fourth deaths yet."

"Excellent point, Baako. I imagine that they reformed the Fatal Five at first to find out about this new virus and the disease it caused; only later did their anger grow as the third and fourth loved one succumbed. I imagine that they needed to plan and share information so bought 5 burner phones. And here's my major insight; I think they bought them as a team, perhaps as a way of bonding on recreating the Fatal Five."

"That sounds plausible but how does it help us?"

"Good question Baako. Remember: **if this is the answer, what is the question?** Imagine them coming out of their great reunion in the cemetery after the second funeral. They'd all be fired up and want to take action immediately by buying all the phones there and then. I imagine one of them had walked past a phone shop on their way to the funeral so took the group back there. So, your job is to start with the date and timing of each funeral. Add on one hour for the wake and Fatal Five reunion and then track the route each person would take to access public transport to get back to their home address. Identify shops selling phones on the way and visit them to see if they sold a set of phones together. Remember, they should have bought 5 phones because one was for Evie Potter who only died later. This major purchase may have occurred after the first, second, third or fourth funeral, but my guess is it'll be the second."

"That'll be like looking for a needle in a haystack. There must be dozens of ways that 5 people could use buses, trains and tubes in London to arrive at a funeral and that's assuming they didn't call an Uber."

"Exactly Pippa; which is why you need to get going immediately and start with the most likely ones; the nearby train stations at Nunhead and Peckham Rye. Remember; we earlier found transactions on their credit cards for train tickets to Nunhead or Peckham Rye on the days of the funerals so it's a reasonable starting point. If you can't find a place near those two stations, spread your net wider."

Once they'd escaped from Painter's office the junior officers started to grumble.

"Another massive pile of work just dumped on us," said Nick.

"He's completely unrealistic. His wild goose chase would take the whole Met a month to do properly, but there's only 3 of us. We'll spend hours plodding the streets and bothering phone shops before he gives up and chooses to follow another hair brained idea."

"Although it would be rather brilliant if it turned out to be correct; just like the Sherlock Holmes stories I read in Afghanistan as a child when I was learning English."

∞

Wednesday 18 November 2020

"How's the investigation into the 5 phones going Nick?"

"Well, sir, there are hundreds of outlets selling pay as you go phones in South London. As you suggested, we started at Ivydale Road and spread out towards the two rail stations. I went to Nunhead, visited 3 shops, explained what we were looking for, but got no luck. Then Pippa phoned me with exciting news and we've regrouped here to share among the team."

Pippa looked as if she was going to jump off her seat.

"It was exactly as you said, sir. I went with Baako to a Vodafone shop near Peckham Rye but had no luck. Then we went to an EE shop, explained what we were looking for and the shop assistant found the details. On Thursday 28 May 2020, in the afternoon after the second funeral, she said 5 people came in and bought 5 pay as you go phones. They got consecutive numbers that I've listed on the whiteboard."

"Could she describe these 5 people?"

"She said there were 3 women and 2 men all in their 20s. She remembers that one woman seemed to be in charge and they all paid cash in turn."

"This is great news and shows the power of taking time to think through a problem rather than rushing into action without a clear plan. Get the numbers over to the tech people. Now we have the phone numbers we can request text messages from the service provider to give us evidence of a conspiracy that we can present to a magistrate to get warrants to search their flats. Show photos of the Famous Five to this shopkeeper and see if she can identify them. We'll meet back here tomorrow at 8 AM to review progress."

Once they had left his office, Painter visited the loo, locked the door and checked to confirm that the 5 phone numbers corresponded with those provided by Tommy. He smiled to himself, safe in the knowledge that he now had two attested police officers who could swear under oath how Painter's team had identified the burner phones.

Thursday 19 November 2020

"Morning everyone. Let's start by asking if the EE shopkeeper could identify our 5 suspects."

"She thought she recognised the photo of Louise, perhaps because she's so striking, but wasn't confident about the others. I'm not sure she'd help our case once it gets to court. She's the sort of person who'd crumble under cross examination."

"That's a bugger but we'll still have the phone numbers and potentially the phones themselves to present to the court. Let's move on to hear what the tech people told you, Pippa."

"They can see loads of messages sent between these numbers, but they're all encrypted as is standard for WhatsApp."

"Can we get them un-encrypted if we give the tech people the physical phones?"

"I asked that, sir but there's no chance. A supercomputer might be able to do it, but we'd have to ask GCHQ. We can't even ask WhatsApp to help because they've set their system up so that even they don't know the codes."

"Just as I thought this case was at last making progress, we get our hopes dashed."

"It's not as bad as it seems, sir. The tech people can see the metadata associated with the messages."

"What does that mean when it's at home?"

"They told me that metadata is really data about data. Metadata includes things like the date and time the message was sent, the phone it was sent by, the phone that received the message and the length of the message."

"We could work with that. Make a long list of all these messages in chronological order and annotate them with the dates of the murders and the dates of the funerals. Meanwhile, I'll go upstairs to see *she who must be obeyed* and ask if we can get GCHQ involved."

* * *

Painter was pleasantly surprised to get an appointment from her PA for that afternoon. Soon, he was glancing at the framed degree certificate before turning right to face his boss's desk.

"Thanks for fitting me into your schedule, ma'am. We've got some developments and could do with your help."

Veronica listened to his story in silence before giving her opinion.

"First, Bill; that's real progress to have found the phone numbers. Did you really just imagine what must have happened and then set out to validate?"

"Yes, ma'am; it's a technique I've used before that I call **if this is the answer what is the question?**"

"Having dealt with the good news, the bad news is that there's no way GCHQ will help us, even if they could. I've been involved with other cases where evidence is encrypted within WhatsApp. GCHQ have taken a decision at a high, policy level that they're not prepared to spend massive amounts of supercomputing time on domestic policing problems. They're also concerned that any evidence they provided would be challenged in court, including requests to examine and test the workings of their supercomputer. So, it's a non-starter I'm afraid."

"Oh well, it was worth a try. My next plan is to tabulate the dates and times of the calls and relate them to the deaths and the funerals. This may give us enough evidence of a conspiracy to ask a magistrate to issue search warrants for the 4 suspects. If we find the 4 phones it would put names to the people who sent and received these messages. It would also show if the timings corresponded to when each of these people had the opportunity to slip poison to each of their victims."

"That sounds a good idea. When you've got the data, go back to Mrs Hall because she's already familiar with the case."

* * *

Mrs Hall listened in silence to Painter's summary of the case. He then showed her the list of times and dates the phones were used and how these corresponded to the dates of the deaths and funerals. He made the point that finding the physical phones would put a name to each of the senders of the WhatsApp messages and would also demonstrate that the suspects had not told the truth when asked if they had access to additional phones. The magistrate then asked some questions:

"Your case has progressed a little since you first asked me for search warrants for the same 4 premises. At that time, you expected to find traces of ricin at one or more sites, but no poison was found, I believe."

"That's correct ma'am."

"Then why should you be given a second warrant to bother these people again? Is this not risking police harassment of innocent citizens?"

"Those negative results for ricin were very helpful to us because we subsequently sought out properties any of the 4 had rented and found ricin there. Your new conditional warrants helped me because the willingness of the individuals to have their kitchens sampled suggested to me that the poison hadn't been prepared there so it must have been made somewhere else."

"You now have evidence of 5 pay as you go phones being bought in the vicinity of Nunhead where these people grew up. But do you have any evidence that these phones are owned by them?"

"No ma'am, but it's very suspicious that the phones

are used on days around each death or funeral. I'm sure the phones belong to our 4 suspects which is why I want to examine their 4 flats to see if the phones are there."

"To me, that seems the wrong way round. As I try to balance the intrusion into the life of innocent citizens with the need for the police to conduct investigations, I'm normally presented with *a priori* evidence."

"We do have evidence ma'am, although I acknowledge that its link to these 4 individuals is circumstantial. It seems to me that the totality of the evidence found so far justifies the request for search warrants given the seriousness of the 4 murders we're investigating but, of course, the decision is yours.

Mrs Hall was silent for a few moments before giving her opinion.

"Your request for 4 search warrants is approved because the seriousness of the crimes outweighs the thin amount of evidence available. However, they will be conditional warrants, as before, which will only be legal if a suspect refuses your polite request to search their property."

* * *

They planned the searches in great detail because Painter didn't want one of the suspects to use their burner phone to advise the others to destroy the evidence. They recruited additional officers for simultaneous evening raids on the 4 flats. In each case the senior officer requested permission to search the property, was denied access and so produced the conditional warrant. Although each flat was small, this all took time, so it was midnight before Painter could finally rest his head on his pillow next to the already sleeping, long suffering Betty.

Saturday 21 November 2020

"We need to get these phones straight away to the lab for DNA and fingerprint testing followed by the tech people to retrieve texts, but I just want to do one thing first."

Painter pulled out his iPhone and dialled 5 consecutive numbers. There was no ringing tone for one number, presumably the phone that belonged to Evie Potter, but the others rang out in turn, warbling within their clear plastic evidence bags.

"That now tells us exactly who's who on that chronological list of communications between the team. We can now work out who sent each message and who received it."

"We'll annotate it all for the team, sir."

"Thanks Pippa. Try to get it to me this afternoon and I'll take it home to read tonight. We next need to plan interviews for the 4 suspects. I've invited Mystic Meg to take part in both the preparation and the interviews themselves. Meet here on Monday at 09:00 for a briefing."

* * *

Painter poured himself a malt, chose a Stan Getz CD and

settled down to read Pippa's paper while humming along to the mellow saxophone.

Chronological lists of messages on WhatsApp with other key relevant information

Tuesday 19 May 2020. Funeral of Albert Harris aged 81. Family all meet up again.

Thursday 28 May 2020. Funeral of Margaret Jones aged 56. We assume the Famous Five reformed on this date because they bought 5 burner phones. First message between the 5 of them. Welcome to our group?

Wednesday 3 June 2020. 4 messages in total from Mandy, Albert, Kevin and then Louise. This is the day that Peter Johnson died. Three messages of condolence with reply of thanks from Louise?

Thursday 4 June 2020. 4 messages in total from Louise, Albert, Kevin and then Mandy. This is the date Evie Potter was taken into hospital. Messages of concern with thanks from Mandy?

Friday 5 June to Monday 8 June 2020. Between 5 and 9 messages each day. Updates on clinical progress?

Tuesday 9 June 2020. 4 messages in total from Louise, Albert, Kevin and then Mandy This is the day that Evie Potter died. Messages of condolence with acknowledgement from Mandy?

Wednesday 17 June 2020. 4 messages. This is the day before the funeral of Peter Johnson. Arranging times to meet?

Thursday 18 June 2020. Funeral of Peter Johnson aged 55. There are no messages so they may have had their discussions face to face after the funeral.

Sunday 21 June 2020. 4 messages. This is the day before the funeral of Evie Potter. Arranging when to meet?

Monday 22 June 2020. Funeral of Evie Potter aged 33. There are no messages so they may have had their discussions face to face after the funeral.

Friday 24 July 2020. 4 messages from Mandy, Louise, Albert then Kevin. This was the date that Mandy Mitchell made a booking on Airbnb for the bungalow in Peacehaven. Simple statement that she'd booked the place followed by acknowledgement of receipt from the others? Absence of prior messages shows that they probably discussed their plan in person. It also shows they're disciplined in their use of WhatsApp - no unnecessary chit-chat, business only.

Saturday 8 August 2020. 4 messages from Mandy, Louise, Albert then Kevin. This is the first day the bungalow at Peacehaven was booked for. Mandy says she's arrived ok? The others offer good luck?

Friday 14 August 2020. 4 messages from Mandy, Louise, Albert then Kevin. This is the penultimate day of the Peacehaven booking. Mandy saying mission accomplished?

Tuesday 18 August 2020. 7 messages from Mandy, Louise, Albert, Kevin, Louise, Albert then Mandy. Negotiating time to meet somewhere (Nunhead cemetery?) for Mandy to give the 3 poisoned food or drink items to the others?

Monday 28 September 2020. One message from Albert to the others. Telling them the poison's been given to Sir John?

Sunday 4 October 2020. One message from Mandy to the others. Telling them the poison's been given to Lord Yeast?

Thursday 8 October 2020. One message from Louise to the others. Telling them the poison's been given to William Randall?

Monday 12 October 2020. One message from Kevin to the others. Telling them the poison's been given to Günter Müller?

Monday 9 November 2020. 1 message from Mandy. The police have contacted me. I'm going with my solicitor. Let her know if they contact you and she'll come to represent you all?

Painter poured himself another glass of malt, selected another Stan Getz CD and sat back to think about other things that could have been said in those messages.

Monday 23 November 2020

They all arrived promptly, keen to find out what was to happen next.

"Welcome Ruth and thanks for your help with this case. The significant development is that we now have the 4 burner phones they used for communications. That allowed us to make this list of dates and times when they shared messages. We can't get to read the actual messages, because they're encrypted, but the timings reveal clear pre-meditation and planning. In going through the list last night, I thought we should search their credit card records to see if they bought rail tickets to meet up on Tuesday 18 August, probably at Nunhead cemetery I would think."

"I'll chase that up sir," said Nick.

"Ruth: we're rather hoping you can get one of these suspects to confess to provide solid evidence to support all our current information which, I'll admit, is circumstantial in nature. To facilitate this, we can offer them the charge of accessory to murder instead of murder itself. But first, can you start by sharing with us your insights into why these 4 upstanding citizens with no previous police record suddenly turned into serial killers?"

"I suggest they've been affected by the chronic unfairness of inequality in our society. Inequality defines and perpetuates a hierarchical social relationship that ranks some people above others, thereby marking the social distance between them. The major differences we have at the moment make social status and class so important that they induce feelings of inferiority which complement the superiority of those in charge. At a time like the pandemic, when we desperately need community cohesion, trust, public spiritedness, mutual support and respect, inequality induces the opposite. As people become more conscious of their status, the whole social structure breaks down and social mobility declines. Evidence from around the world shows that societies that are more unequal have worse mental and physical health and show poorer levels of child development and well-being. Inequality causes chronic stress, gets under the skin of citizens, gets into their minds, shaping their behaviour. This social stress also manifests in your area, by producing more antisocial behaviour, more people sent to prison and higher murder rates.

With this as background, it's not difficult to imagine what happened to the people you've identified. They're the little people in our society who've had enough and finally snapped after the deaths of 4 people they loved. People don't complain about the fact they're being exploited and put in harm's way because it's normalised; poor people are always the ones who do face to face jobs, exposing them to infections or complaints from angry customers. Meanwhile, their managers sit in an office analysing the data showing staff productivity. With Covid, those managers moved to the safety of their own living rooms and gave instructions over Zoom. Anthropologists call this social silence, where people without autonomy learn never to mention their exploitation."

"Do you think they form a coherent and complete group?"

"If you're trying to find a group of people with close connections, remember a tribe can be defined not just by who's an insider but also who's left out. These 5 were selected by opportunity of adjacent houses where they grew up, but was there someone else as well?"

"We'll bear that in mind as the investigation progresses but focus on the 4 who remain alive to begin with. Who do you recommend we interview first?"

"Like a pack of lions circling a herd of antelope, we should prey on the weakest. That's Kevin, because he's only recently had the courage to leave the bosom of his mother and start fending for himself in the big wide world."

"Right then Nick, over to you. Check that Kevin Jones is at his place of work today because I want the squad car and uniformed officer to be seen clearly by all his workmates as he's taken away. If he refuses to come voluntarily, arrest him on suspicion of the murder of Günter Müller and handcuff him."

* * *

Kevin looked scared as he was led into the interview room and sat waiting. Eventually his solicitor arrived and Painter could begin:

"For the benefit of the tape, the people present are Inspector Bill Painter, Dr Ruth Barnes, Kevin Jones and Miss Olivia Wright, his solicitor. I have explained that Mr Jones will be interviewed under caution and that his replies may be presented in court."

"Are you medically qualified, Dr Barnes?" asked Olivia.

"No, I'm not."

"Then may I ask what subject your doctorate was awarded in?"

"Psychology," Ruth replied and then took over the questioning firmly, leaving no doubt as to who was in charge.

"Kevin, we want to make it clear to you that you're facing the possibility of a very serious charge, that of murder. If convicted, you would be sentenced to spend many years in prison."

"That would only apply if my client was found guilty," added Olivia.

"That's true and we should also agree that it's not the only possible charge, because Kevin might be considered an accessory to murder which is much less serious. Let's explore now what we think your contribution was to this enterprise. Let's go back in time. You first met the others at primary school where you played together in the garden of your adjacent houses, spilling over to enjoy the space of the cemetery. There's nothing wrong with that."

Kevin managed a little smile of acknowledgment towards Ruth.

"You then went to secondary school where you only got GCSEs. Is that correct?"

"Yes, it is."

"In contrast, the two girls achieved A levels when they went to different schools, didn't they?"

"Yes, they did."

"We think they were the brains behind the scheme not you. Your mistake was to get mixed up in their plan. This is not your fault."

Kevin sat up and looked as if the weight of the world was beginning to lift from his shoulders. Painter was reminded of watching Betty's baking when her whisked egg whites turned from liquid to stiff peaks resembling miniature white mountains.

"But, as it stands, you face the same very serious charge as do the girls."

Kevin slumped back down in his chair. The interview that had started so well had now slowed down.

"We know what the group has done apart from a few details. From our experience of other similar cases, we also know what happens next; one of the group will tell us those details and Inspector Painter here will recommend a lesser charge than murder for that person. Factors can be taken into account and he'll ask the judge to be lenient towards that person because they've helped bring the case to a conclusion quickly and so reduced the cost to the justice system. The question for you is, are you going to help the Inspector now and get a short sentence or do you want to wait for one of the others to do it?"

Kevin looked towards Olivia who announced:

"My client deserves a short refreshment break now."

* * *

After 15 minutes, Olivia returned to the interview room followed by Kevin.

Painter restarted the tape and Ruth resumed her questioning:

"Kevin: when we stopped, we were discussing the potential charges you could face. The question for you is, are you going to help the Inspector by answering some questions now? This will have the clear understanding between us, your solicitor and anyone who listens to this tape that you were only an accessory to murder, not someone who should be charged with murder itself."

Kevin hesitated for a moment, looked at Olivia and replied in a weak voice:

"No comment."

Painter then intervened.

"Kevin, you gave us the details of your mobile phone when we first interviewed you. We asked if you had access to a second phone, a pay as you go perhaps and you denied this. We now know this was a lie. The burner phone we found in your flat has your fingerprints and your DNA all over it. We have all the text messages you sent or received showing you were a key member of the group. When we produce the phone in court the jury will not be inclined to believe anything else you say. The charge you face is so serious that I'm going to repeat our offer one more time. This isn't looking good for you so, if you know anything, now's the time to tell me. Will you cooperate with us on the understanding that you will not be prosecuted for murder?"

Kevin glanced at Olivia before replying:

"No comment."

"Inspector Painter, my client has clearly indicated to you, as recorded here, that he is innocent of the serious crimes you have mentioned. Unless you wish to charge him here and now, this interview is terminated and we intend to leave New Scotland Yard."

Once Kevin and Olivia had left, Painter and Ruth moved to the viewing room to join the others.

"I won't disguise my disappointment that Kevin didn't roll over and help us. He's assuming we won't be able to prove him guilty. We'll see about that. Bring on the next one which I assume is Albert."

On receiving a nod from Ruth, Nick set off for Regent's Park in a squad car, but not before telling Painter that all members of the Fatal Four had bought rail tickets to travel to Nunhead on 18 August.

* * *

Albert looked from side to side as he was led into the interview room. He didn't have long to wait for his solicitor, allowing Painter to begin the proceedings:

"For the tape, the people present are Inspector Bill Painter, Dr Ruth Barnes, Albert Harris and Miss Olivia Wright, his solicitor. I have explained that Mr Harris will be interviewed under caution and that his replies may be presented in court."

Ruth then asked a series of questions, similar to those she had asked Kevin.

"Albert, I want to make clear that you're facing the possibility of a very serious charge, that of murder. If convicted, you would be sentenced to spend many years in prison."

"That would only apply if my client was found guilty," added Olivia.

"I agree, but Albert is running this risk. However, murder is not the only possible charge, because he might be considered an accessory to murder which is much less serious. I want to help you by exploring now what we think your contribution was to this enterprise by going back in time. You first met the others at primary school, I believe?"

"Yes, that's right."

"Did you often play together in the garden of your adjacent houses, spilling over to enjoy the space of the cemetery as children?"

"Yes, we did."

"Let me emphasise that there's no crime in doing that."

Albert gave a little smile to Ruth but said nothing.

"You then went to secondary school where you got GCSEs but didn't stay on to do A levels. Is that correct?"

"Yes, it is."

"In contrast, both girls achieved A levels when they went to different schools, didn't they?"

"Yes, they did."

"We think they were the brains behind the scheme not you. Your mistake was to get mixed up in their plan. This is not your fault."

Like Kevin, Albert looked as if the weight of the world was beginning to lift from his shoulders.

"But, as it stands, you face the same very serious charge as do the girls."

Albert's eyes darted from left to right and back again as if he were hunting for something important. Painter was reminded of his daughter stranded on stage during a school play desperately trying to locate her cue cards.

"We know what the group has done apart from a few minor details. From our experience of other cases like this, we also know what happens next. One member of the group will tell us those details and Inspector Painter here will recommend a lesser charge than murder for that person. Factors can be taken into account and he'll ask the judge to be lenient towards that person because they've helped bring the case to a conclusion quickly. The question for you is, are you going to help the Inspector now and get a short sentence or do you want to wait for one of the others to do it?"

Albert looked towards Olivia who announced:

"My client requests a short refreshment break."

* * *

After 15 minutes, Olivia returned to the interview room followed by Albert.

Painter restarted the tape and Ruth resumed her questioning:

"Albert: when we paused for a break, we were discussing the potential charges you could face. The question for you now is, are you going to help the Inspector by answering some questions? There's a clear understanding between us, your solicitor and anyone who listens to this tape that you were only an accessory to murder, not someone who should be charged with murder itself."

Albert hesitated for a moment, looked at Olivia and replied in a weak voice:

"No comment."

It was then Painter's turn to speak.

"Albert, when we first interviewed you, you gave us the details of your mobile phone. We asked if you had access to a second phone, but you denied this. We now know this was not true. The burner phone we found in your flat is covered in your fingerprints and your DNA. We also have all the messages that the phone sent or received so we can demonstrate your active participation in the group. When we produce the pay-as-you go phone in court the jury will not be inclined to believe anything else you say. For example, when our barrister asks you under oath why you bought a rail ticket to travel to Nunhead on 18 August, what will you reply? The charge you face is so serious that I'm going to repeat our offer to you one more time. This isn't looking good for you so, if you know anything, now's the time to tell me. Will you cooperate with us on the understanding that you'll not be prosecuted for murder?"

Albert glanced at Olivia and then replied:

"No comment."

"Inspector Painter, my client has clearly indicated to you, as recorded here, that he's innocent of the serious crimes you have mentioned. Unless you wish to charge him here and now, this interview is terminated and we intend to leave New Scotland Yard."

Painter and Ruth joined the others in the viewing room once Albert and Olivia had left,

"He also assumes we won't be able to prove him guilty. Bring on the next one which I assume, Ruth, is Louise."

Nick set off for Islington in a squad car.

* * *

Louise was strikingly attractive as always, but looked ill at ease as she was led into the interview room. She held her handbag tight as if it were trying to pull away; just like a puppy on a lead. Olivia soon arrived, allowing Painter to begin the proceedings:

"For the tape, the people present are Inspector Bill Painter, Dr Ruth Barnes, Louise Johnson and Miss Olivia Wright, her solicitor. I've explained that Miss Johnson is being interviewed under caution and that her replies may be presented in court."

Ruth started asking her series of questions:

"Louise, I want to make clear that you're facing the possibility of a very serious charge, that of murder. If convicted, you would be sentenced to spend many years in prison."

"That would only happen if my client was found guilty," added Olivia.

"I agree, but Louise is taking this risk, not you, Miss Wright. I want to explain to Louise that murder is not the only possible charge, because she might be considered an accessory to murder which is much less serious. I want to help her consider this possibility by exploring now what we think her contribution was to this enterprise by going back in time. You first met the others at primary school, I believe?"

"Yes, I did."

"Is it true that you often played together in the garden of your adjacent houses, spilling over to enjoy the space of the cemetery as children?"

"Yes, we did that."

"Let me emphasise that's not a crime."

Louise gave a little smile to Ruth but said nothing.

"You then went to secondary school where you got A levels. Is that correct?"

"Yes, it is."

"You then had the experience of going to 4 funerals of people you'd known since childhood. That must have been awful."

"Yes, it was."

"Your childhood group then cooked up a plan that you got mixed up in. We don't think you were the brains behind this plan. We don't think it's your fault."

Louise smiled again at Ruth and visibly relaxed.

"But, as things stand, you face the same very serious charge as do the others."

Louise's eyes darted across to her solicitor, but Olivia said nothing.

"We know what the group has done apart from a few minor points. From our experience of cases like this, we also know what's likely to happen next. One member of the group will tell us the details we need and Inspector Painter will recommend they face a lesser charge than murder. Factors can be taken into account and he'll ask the judge to be lenient towards the person whose information helped bring the case to a conclusion quickly. The question for you is, are you going to help the Inspector now and get a short sentence or do you want to wait for one of the others to do it?"

Louise stared down at the table as if the answer she was seeking was written into the Formica top.

Ruth pressed her some more:

"Louise, you've already given your body in support of their plan; please don't give up the rest of your life as well. You're an attractive young woman now but would be middle aged by the time you were let out and prison does nothing for the complexion."

Louise again looked towards Olivia who announced:

"My client needs a short refreshment break."

* * *

After 20 minutes, Olivia returned to the interview room followed by Louise.

Painter restarted the tape and Ruth resumed:

"Louise: when we paused for a break, we were discussing the potential charges you could face. What you now have to consider is, are you going to help the Inspector by answering a few questions? There's a clear understanding between us, your solicitor and anyone who later listens to this tape that you were only an accessory to murder, not someone who should be charged with murder itself."

Louise hesitated for a moment, looked at Olivia and replied weakly:

"No comment."

It was Painter's turn to speak.

"Louise, at our first interview, you gave us the details of your mobile phone. We asked if you had access to a second phone, but you denied this. We now know this wasn't true. The burner phone we found in your flat has your fingerprints and your DNA all over it. We also have records showing the multiple messages sent from and received by your phone, which prove you were an active member of the group. When we produce the pay-as-you go phone in court the jury will not be inclined to believe anything else you say. What will you reply when our barrister asks you under oath why you bought a rail ticket to travel to Nunhead on 18 August? Whatever you say, he'll tell the jury that was the date when Mandy handed over items contaminated with ricin to you all, using the messages sent on WhatsApp to support this conclusion. Who do you think the jury will believe once we've proven that you lied about the burner phone? This isn't looking good for you so, if you know anything, now's the time to tell me. The charge you face is so serious that I'm going to repeat our offer to you one last time. Will you cooperate with us on the understanding that you'll not be prosecuted for murder?"

Louise looked towards Olivia before replying:

"No comment."

Painter came back with an additional unscripted question:

"How was the tea my colleagues provided during the break?"

Louise paused before replying:

"To be frank, it was rather weak."

"A bit like your answers to my questions, then," shot back Painter.

Hidden away behind the two-way mirror, Nick whispered to Pippa: "the pressure's getting to him; he's starting to lose his cool."

Back in the interview room, Olivia took control:

"Inspector Painter, my client has clearly stated, as recorded here, that she's innocent of the serious crimes you've mentioned. Unless you wish to charge her, this interview is over and we intend to leave New Scotland Yard."

Painter and Ruth joined the others in the viewing room once Louise and Olivia had left,

"You almost had her there, Ruth. I could feel her deciding whether to take the easy option. Like the others, she assumes we won't be able to prove her guilty. Bring on the last one, who we think is the brains behind this plot and the person who brewed up the poison."

Nick set off for the Barbican in a squad car.

* * *

Painter took his leave from the group and went to the men's room. Sitting quietly in a cubicle he could feel the pressure to get a confession building up within him. He knew that if he dropped a bollock on this case the Commissioner might ask for the other one. He'd done all he could; it would now fall to the last suspect to give him an easy route to success. Tentatively, he stood up, looked at his pale face in the mirror as he washed his hands and walked out, ready to face the music.

Mandy looked confident as she was led into the interview room.

"For the tape, the people present are Inspector Bill Painter, Dr Ruth Barnes, Mandy Mitchell and Miss Olivia Wright, her solicitor. I've explained that Miss Mitchell is being interviewed under caution and that her replies may be presented in court."

Ruth started asking her series of questions:

"Mandy, I want to make clear that you're facing the possibility of a very serious charge, that of murder. If convicted, you would be sentenced to spend many years in prison."

"Only if my client was found guilty," added Olivia.

"I agree, but Mandy's taking that risk. I want to explain to Mandy that murder's not the only possible charge, because she could be considered to have diminished responsibility which would lessen the sentence. I want to help her consider these possibilities by exploring what's happened recently. In summary, you had the terrible experience of going to 4 funerals of people you cared about. In response, your childhood group got itself involved in a complicated plan to seek retribution."

Mandy's eyes looked across to her solicitor, but Olivia said nothing.

"We know what the group has done apart from a few minor points. We have your 4 burner phones and the multiple WhatsApp messages you used to communicate with each other. From our experience of cases like this, we can anticipate what's likely to happen next. One member of the group will tell us the details we need and Inspector Painter will recommend they face a lesser charge than murder. Factors can be taken into account and he'll ask the judge to be lenient towards the person who helped bring the case to a conclusion. The question for you is, are you going to help the Inspector now before one of the others does it?"

Mandy stared straight forwards at the wall opposite her.

Ruth pressed her further:

"Mandy, I know this must have been tough on you because one of those 4 funerals was for your sister. This came on top of everything else the others had to bear so you can make a case for diminished responsibilities compared to them."

Mandy continued to stare straight ahead.

"Mandy, don't throw away the rest of your life. You'd be middle aged before they let you out of prison. Will you explore options with us?"

Mandy again looked towards Olivia before saying in a clear voice:

"No comment."

It was then Painter's turn to speak.

"Mandy, at your very first interview, you gave us the details of your mobile. We asked if you had access to a second phone, but you denied this. We now know this was a lie. The burner phone we found in your flat has your fingerprints and your DNA on it. We also have records of the messages sent from and received by your phone. When we produce the pay-as-you go phone in court the jury will not be inclined to believe anything else you say. When our barrister asks you under oath why you bought a rail ticket to travel to Nunhead on 18 August, what will you reply? Whatever you say, he'll tell the jury that was the date when you handed over items contaminated with ricin to the others, using the messages sent on WhatsApp to support this. Our investigation has uncovered so much information that the jury will realise why you're not giving straight answers to simple questions. The charge you face is so serious that I'm going to repeat our offer to you one more time. This isn't looking good for you so, if you know anything, now's the time to tell me. Will you cooperate with us on the understanding that any prosecution would be under diminished responsibilities?"

Mandy glanced at Olivia and then smiled as she replied:

"No comment."

"I'm going to offer you and your solicitor a brief refreshment break."

Mandy looked at Olivia before replying:

"No thank you; that won't be necessary."

Olivia took over control of the process, challenging Painter to put up or shut up:

"Inspector Painter, my client has clearly stated, and recorded for the tape, that she's innocent of the serious crimes you've mentioned. Unless you wish to charge her immediately, this interview is over and we will leave New Scotland Yard."

As they were leaving, Painter asked Olivia for a quiet

word off the record and they moved out into the corridor.

"Are you happy representing all 4 suspects here? Are you allowed to do so? Shouldn't they each have their own solicitor to advise them about their individual interests?"

"I stepped in because I'd previously represented one of the 4 and she told me that none of the others had a solicitor. I've explained to each of them that I can only represent them during these initial phases of investigation. If you decide to prosecute, I'd have a conflict of interest and the guidelines do indeed state that each person should have their own advisor. Does that answer your question?"

"Yes, it does, thank you. My next question concerns the likely outcome here. You must know that we have a strong case. Are you proud of protecting murderers? How does that sit with your professional approach to justice for our 4 victims and their families?"

"I can see why you wanted this conversation off the record, Inspector, because if you said that on the tape, I would file an official complaint. My role in the criminal justice process is to protect my clients from the crimes police officers imagine they've committed. Your role is to produce incontrovertible evidence sufficient to convince a jury that a crime has been committed by those clients. I note you've no evidence of such crimes and haven't charged any of the 4, so suggest you get back to work instead of trying to intimidate me."

With that, Olivia turned on her heel and walked calmly but confidently out of the building.

Painter joined the others in the viewing room:

"Good try, Ruth, but Mandy knows we think she's the person who brewed up the poison so it would be difficult to avoid charging her with murder, even if she claimed diminished responsibilities. She's going to take her chance with the jury."

Tuesday 24 November 2020

As the large hand became almost vertical, it was time for Painter to climb upstairs, be ushered into the office, glance at the framed degree certificate and turn right to face Veronica. He was gaining a grudging respect for her but still felt she did herself no favours by having such a short haircut.

"I need to brief you on progress, ma'am and get your advice on asking the CPS to approve prosecuting the 4 suspects for murder. We've got clear evidence of premeditation and conspiracy so will be able to prosecute under the rules of joint enterprise."

Veronica listened as he walked through the cases and the voluminous evidence they had accumulated.

"You've brought clarity to these cases that were so confusing to begin with. There's no doubt in my mind that they're guilty as hell and should all go down for murder. Your intuitive way of finding the burner phones was remarkable and is still being talked about in the canteen. However, my role is to act as devil's advocate by suggesting to you that the CPS may say all the evidence is simply circumstantial."

"I agree with that ma'am, which is why I tried to get a confession out of any one of them, but their solicitor was obstructive. When the case is put before the jury the defendants will find it very difficult to explain why they bought burner phones and why their messages were sent exactly on the days that our 4 victims were poisoned or when they attended funerals. We've also got the booking of the bungalow in Peacehaven and the finding of ricin there."

"Continuing my role as devil's advocate, have you considered that the defence may merely say that it's not a crime to have a pay as you go phone and use it to communicate with people you haven't seen for years since you were at school with them? You can't get the content of the messages so can't prove they had anything to do with the murders. The defence may simply sit back and tell the jury it's the prosecution's job to prove a crime was committed, not their job to prove their clients' innocence."

"You're correct ma'am in saying that's a likely strategy for the defence, but I'm saying that a jury won't be taken for fools; they know how suspicious everything looks."

"That's why I fear the defence may not call any of the 4 defendants to the stand. They'd say that innocent citizens don't have to explain the details of their personal lives. I'll give permission for you to forward the papers but, on balance, I think you need to be prepared for the CPS to say they won't authorise a prosecution."

Painter stomped downstairs uttering under his

breath the alternative name police officers gave the CPS: **Couldn't Prosecute Satan**.

* * *

After submitting all the paperwork with his request that the 4 should be prosecuted for murder so that a jury could decide, Painter had to wait for a decision from the CPS. Time dragged on as he occupied himself with routine cases. He was beginning to think the CPS would never put him out of his misery when his iPhone rang:

Frederick Butterworth

"Hello Fred; how are you?"

"I'm ok thanks Bill. How did you get on with those 4 poisonings I referred to you?"

"We have suspects and are waiting for the CPS to tell us if we can take them to court."

"Don't hold your breath; you know what CPS stands for don't you?"

"Yes, I do Fred and I agree they're too cautious, but there's nothing we can do about it. How can I help you today?"

"Well, I've got another one for you with a flag saying you're to be contacted if the person dies. Man of 66 found dead at home. Paramedics think its poisoning, so I'll text you all the details. It's not a VIP this time; it's his son who's famous, so mind how you go."

* * *

Painter picked up the Northern line at Embankment. Throughout the journey he wondered how this new case could fit in with the previous 4. Why would the Fatal Four commit another murder when they knew in no uncertain terms that Painter had them in the frame for 4 others? Mystic Meg had said that there might be another team member, so was he or she behind it? Alternatively, had Painter got it all wrong and the evidence implicating the Fatal Five was simply the product of his fertile imagination finding connections between circumstantial pieces of information?

The tube pulled into Camden Town station and he had time to take stock of all the thoughts racing around his head. Could this new case be completely unconnected with the previous 4? Painter looked again at the home address he'd been given for the victim; if this one was unconnected, it must be a coincidence that his son was a VIP and the house backed onto Highgate Cemetery.

He got out at Belsize Park, located the pathologist at the Royal Free Hospital and listened intently to his description of the case:

"Mr George Eastwood was a 68-year-old widower

living alone since his wife died two years ago. A neighbour raised the alarm when she hadn't seen Mr Eastwood around. Apparently, he was getting a bit forgetful and confused. The neighbour volunteered that Mr Eastwood had recently become preoccupied with the rats in his small garden; it seems that they're quite common in Highgate Cemetery. He had a past medical history of hypertension for which he was taking valsartan. There's a flag on his record saying you wish to be informed if this person dies, especially if poisoning is suspected."

"That's right. I recognise the name as one of the people prescribed valsartan by a medical practice in Harley Street that was part of another case."

"Harley Street, eh? Well, I gather that his son Engelbert Eastwood is a well know chat show host on television, so you may have some interest from the press to deal with."

"Was he poisoned?"

"Yes, he was. The police found the body in the upstairs bathroom with extensive bleeding, enough for him to have exsanguinated within minutes. I conducted a full post mortem examination which revealed pale kidneys and liver, typical of acute bleeding. He had a large gastric ulcer as the source of the bleeding. Toxicology revealed extremely high levels of warfarin. In conclusion, my report gives the cause of death as haemorrhage secondary to warfarin poisoning. I suggest this was accidentally ingested during one or more attempts to put down rat poison, a packet of which was found in his kitchen cupboard."

"Did the toxicology exclude poisoning with ricin?"

"Yes, it did."

Painter set off back to New Scotland Yard relieved that he didn't have another murder to add to the series, because the VIP was not an industrialist and the poison used was not ricin. The unfortunate case of Mr Eastwood would not require him to change his hypothesis about the other 4 murders and wouldn't require him to update the documents he'd sent to the CPS. He just needed them to make a decision...

Thursday 26 November 2020

Painter's morning started out normally with a bus journey on the 277 to Mile End followed by a ride on the District line to Westminster.

He had no sooner arrived than an email flashed up on his computer. Tentatively, he clicked on the message entitled: **response from CPS re case 4172359**.

The CPS acknowledges that there is a compelling story here based on circumstance, but we are concerned about insufficient hard evidence.

We are also concerned that a competent defence lawyer would tell the jury that it is not a crime to own pay as you go mobile phones or to use them to stay in contact with old school friends. He or she would then say that his or her clients had no case to answer and decline to put them in the witness stand, thereby avoiding cross-examination. The defence would rest on the need for the prosecution to prove its case, not for the defence to prove innocence. Overall, we feel there is a substantial risk that a jury would acquit the defendants under these circumstances, and so cannot authorise the prosecution to proceed.

We know this decision will come as a disappointment to the investigating team. We invite you to return to us if more information becomes concrete; for exam-

ple, if a change in the law forces service providers to de-encrypt WhatsApp messages.

* * *

Painter poured himself a large glass of malt and selected *Lady Sings the Blues.* While indulging his miserable mood, he needed to think if there were any points he'd missed or anything he could have done better during the investigation, but first he'd give himself a break by starting with what he got right.

He got the abbreviation correct; **Couldn't Prosecute Satan** summed them up nicely. He agreed that the information was mainly circumstantial, but why not put it before a jury? How could the defence explain away the detection of the ricin in the bungalow in Peacehaven? How would they explain the suspects lying about not having a second phone and then his officers finding, hidden in their flats, 4 secret mobiles each with the fingerprints and DNA of one suspect? A jury would show common sense, see from the metadata that these people had texted each other messages about the murders and take their refusal to give access to the content of those messages as an acceptance of guilt. Honest people help the police with enquiries and would gladly reveal what the WhatsApp messages say if they were innocuous. Not for the first time, Painter thought that the French inquisitorial system, where an investigating magistrate finds all the facts prior to prosecution, is superior to our adversarial system where lawyers play games.

He also managed his secret weapon well. He'd deployed Tommy at exactly the right time, saving the investigation many hours of searching the wrong shops selling burner phones. His explanation of how he'd imagined the villains had these phones and prioritised the shops near the railway stations for searching had, according to Veronica, gone down as a canteen room legend. He'd achieved his objective while minimising the risk that Tommy represented to Painter, his career and his pension, with two attested police officers able to swear under oath how they decided to visit local shops selling phones. He took another swig of the malt, then forced back a grim smile as he acknowledged the investigation had ultimately failed to get a conviction so he now had to consider what he could have done differently.

He could have paid more attention to Baako's suggestion about family connections. If only he'd twigged that the term *family* could have a wider interpretation to include all the people who shared someone's formative years, he could have found the link to the school in Nunhead earlier. They'd followed standard procedures, but why do investigations normally go back as far as secondary schools but not include primary schools? Perhaps this was a change to suggest to Veronica for the future, although he knew he'd get pushback because information prior to starting work was not available electronically and so was time consuming and expensive to obtain.

Was it a question of who the messenger was? Did he fail to pay attention because Baako came from a different country? Painter thought back and recognised that he'd initially been underwhelmed at the prospect of what she could contribute to his investigation; he'd try not to make the same mistake again. Was it also because Baako was female? A previous Superintendent had told him he was too dismissive of females in the workplace and did not seem impressed when he offered **providing comfort to grieving relatives** as a major advantage of having female officers in the force. She would have gone ballistic if he'd added **making tea for senior officers**. Yes, this was an area he needed to work on in the future. Mind you, although Baako's suggestion had turned out to be correct, the input from the other female in the team, Pippa, about poisonings in literature had been useless. He took another sip of whisky before acknowledging that he was the one who'd asked Pippa to create the list, so he couldn't really blame her.

What about the beautiful Louise? He'd almost got onto her as a villain at an early stage when Pippa got the hint that the secretary was having an affair with Mr Randall. He should remember for future cases that if a man of his age could find such a woman attractive, then other men could have their heads turned too. Painter could also have suspected something funny was going on when the man, who was in charge of London Transport, told his wife he needed a car to collect him each morning, despite the ready availability of a route on public transport. He should have realised the man had an exalted opinion of himself and worked out that this extended to assuming that his female staff would want to sleep with him.

The whole case also illustrated how the timing of appearance of information could influence the narrative because, if the flagged man had poisoned himself, as well as rats, earlier in the course of the investigations, the pattern of ricin poisoning wouldn't have been so apparent. How could he possibly know which deaths were related and which were coincidental? How could he tell in the future if individual deaths were part of a conspiracy before the full set of them had been revealed? Would he ever be able to do this in time to prevent the last murder in a planned series? The Fatal Five only aimed to kill 4 people in total, consistent with the doctrine of an eye for an eye that was drummed into them in childhood. However, if there had been a fifth, could Painter have stopped it?

The Billie Holliday CD came to an end and Painter selected another, more upbeat this time, to help him move on from looking backwards. Thelonious Monk was one of his favourites and the exquisite piano playing in *Introspection* allowed Painter to reflect on the broader setting of the case. The news programmes were full of how people won't be able to cope once inflation, that he remembered well, reared its ugly head again. No doubt the corpulent Bank of England Governor- who could easily afford to tighten his belt- would urge pay restraint but, as always, this would apply to ordinary people not to the bankers or CEOs the Governor had control over. It was one rule for them and another for the rest of us as unfairness continued to dominate the little people as always. Mind you, one of the rich victims, Sir John, had declined to use legal ways to reduce his inheritance tax payment but had kept this generosity quiet. Perhaps other rich people did the same without seeking publicity. Bill Gates was working hard to give most of his fortune to charity and was recruiting other billionaires to the cause. This was highly desirable, but should it be encouraged by carrot or stick? A carrot could take the form of a matching contribution from the government to the billionaire's cause. A stick would alter the tax system to tax wealth unless millionaires agreed to donate voluntarily. Would either of these changes influence citizens bent on retribution for obvious unfairness? Would the Fatal Five have reprieved Sir John if they'd known the contents of his last will and testament? Painter took another swig of malt whisky and concluded that they only attacked Sir John because they had access; they were opportunists getting back at some capitalists, not class warriors systematically killing all rich people.

Painter poured himself a final glass of malt and enjoyed the warm feeling as the precious liquid flowed down his gullet. When the CD finished, he quelled the magnificent music machine and made his way unsteadily upstairs hoping that he would now sleep well despite the day's disappointing news.

Monday 30 November 2020

Painter's office phone rang and he heard that a solicitor wished to speak to him. He asked for the call to be put through as he pulled over a clean sheet of paper to make notes.

"Thank you, Inspector Painter, for agreeing to talk to me. My name is Dominic Fitzhugh and I am the senior partner in Fitzhugh, Grimes based in the West End. Are you amenable to a hypothetical discussion completely off the record about a case I understand you're working on?"

"I'm always happy to discuss areas of mutual interest informally, but I have several cases on the go at the moment, so could you give me more details?"

"Everything I am about to say is off the record, without prejudice and would be inadmissible in court."

"I can agree to that."

"Then I believe you have recently interviewed 4 people about the unfortunate deaths of 4 males and are considering serious charges."

"That's correct."

"I was approached on Friday by a new client. After spending the weekend thinking about what I was told I suspect there may be mutual benefit in my client revealing the few facts they know under the strict understanding that serious charges with the potential for a custodial sentence would not be sought."

"You'll be aware that we don't have the USA system of plea bargaining but I'm always open to requesting that judges show leniency to one suspect in a group to reflect the help they've given us in bringing a trial to a swift conclusion. In my experience, judges are keen to minimise costs for the public purse by having shorter trials where the evidence is clear and unambiguous."

"Then I suggest we meet to explore, without commitment on either side, whether any information my client may possess may lead you to make such a recommendation. I suggest we avoid New Scotland Yard or my office at this stage. Are you familiar with the outdoor coffee shop at the Albert Memorial?"

"Yes, I am. It's in the open air and it would be easy to have the off the record discussion we both seek without anyone eavesdropping. Would 2 PM today be convenient?"

"Yes, that's good for me."

"Then I suggest that the first one there gets the coffee."

"Forgive me, Inspector, but I suggest we should each purchase our own refreshments. If the case comes to court, I wouldn't want a barrister to suggest that I had attempted to bribe you."

* * *

It wasn't difficult to spot Dominic Fitzhugh; a man in his mid 50s wearing a dark suit and tie contrasted easily with the casually dressed tourists. He had already commandeered an isolated table and was nursing a coffee, so Painter got his usual cappuccino with skimmed milk and introduced himself.

"Before we start, I must confirm my understanding that everything we say is off the record."

"Yes, I can confirm that, so how can I help? "

"I find myself in a somewhat uncomfortable position because I gather another solicitor sat in on the interviews of all 4 people, including my client. That's against guidelines because each person deserves advice based on their personal circumstances."

"I agree and did have a quiet word with the solicitor who said she was just stepping in temporarily and would hand over if formal charges were laid."

"Can I ask if you plan to charge any of the 4?"

"You know I can't answer that, but I can tell you that papers have been sent to the CPS and your client runs the risk of being prosecuted under the rules of joint enterprise with the most severe possible charge being murder."

"From what I've been told, my client would not deserve that. To avoid a miscarriage of justice my client has instructed me to negotiate informally to see if providing some factual information might lead you to seek leniency from the judge."

"I can't make any promises but am happy to proceed on that assumption. Obviously, any charges laid would depend upon exactly what contribution your client made to the overall scheme. We already suspect that some of the 4 played leading roles while others were just supportive. I could give you a better indication if you told me your client's name."

"I really couldn't disclose that at this point."

"What about telling me if they're male or female?"

The solicitor paused before replying:

"Again, that would be improper, but I'll put your comments back to my client and let you know what he says."

Painter covered his tendency to smile at this reply by draining his coffee cup.

"In that case, I think I can assure you that we expect any charges for your client to be on the milder side of those being considered. Can I invite you and your client to record an interview under caution at New Scotland Yard where I will state at the outset that we're not looking to prosecute your client for murder?"

"Having explained the concept of joint enterprise prosecutions to my client and given a warning of what could happen, I think what you just said would provide some comfort. Once you've received answers to your questions, I think you'll agree that his role was minor and unwitting. Can I also request that the interview is conducted in the presence of the female doctor who asked the questions last time? My client felt that she understood the situation well."

"Yes, I was thinking along the same lines. Here's my card with my mobile number; call me to arrange a date and time."

Tuesday 1 December 2020

Painter briefed his junior officers at their 9 AM meeting and outlined the next steps.

"I've telephoned Mystic Meg to make sure she's still on board and free to join in the interview. I've briefed *she who must be obeyed* and got her permission to go back to the CPS with any new information we get. I now need to give you all a tutorial on the possible charges we could ask for. To be charged with murder, a suspect should be of sound mind and have an intention to kill or cause serious harm. There are partial defences with diminished responsibility being the only one relevant to our cases. Duress is not an acceptable defence, so the boys can't claim they were bullied by the girls. There is then the consideration of who among the group is the principal party, or co-principal parties, and who should be considered an accessory to murder. Pippa: who would you suggest for these roles?"

"Well sir, I don't know the exact criteria, but Mandy the catering lady could be our principal party. She prepared the poison. She booked the bungalow in Peacehaven. We believe she concealed the poison within the 4 items of food, one intended for each victim. All of these demonstrate premeditation, so I'd vote for her."

"I agree with you. Mandy is what lawyers call the guiding mind that sees the whole picture and puts in place the various steps needed to deliver the overall outcome. How would you assess Louise, the attractive secretary?"

"She was key to getting close enough to her boss to deliver the poisoned food. Ruth told us that her commitment to giving her body to the cause may have been influential in persuading the others to come on board. I guess she's either a co-principal party or an accessory."

"I agree with you and it'll be interesting to see which way the CPS jumps. What about Kevin?"

"He delivered the poisoned food item that we believe was a gummy bear. He must have known the consequences of his actions because 3 people had died by then. This shows clear premeditation. On balance, I'd go for him as an accessory."

"Again, I agree. His contribution was important, but it was mainly through the delivery of the item prepared by Mandy. What about Albert?"

"I'd put him in the same category as Kevin; accessory to murder because all he did was deliver the poisoned food item, although we've no idea what that was."

"True, but there's one other fact to consider. Albert was involved in Case 1 and could claim that he didn't really know that Sir John would die. That claim can't be made by Kevin, who was involved with Case 4. The reason this is important is that we need the information and statement from our suspect to give us enough to go back to the CPS. In return, the solicitor for this person will be looking for mitigation. We know the person is male; what could we offer to Kevin or to Albert?"

"Could we offer them both manslaughter instead of murder as well as leniency for helping us with the case?"

"We could do that for Albert but I'm not sure the CPS would wear it for Kevin when 3 deaths had occurred already. The solicitor will know this and will want us to pull something out of the hat if he's going to allow his client to make an incriminating statement. Let's hope the solicitor hasn't developed cold feet and does phone me to accept the invitation to an interview. It would be easier if his client is Albert but we must prepare for it to be either Albert or Kevin. I'll be meeting with Ruth to do just that."

Thursday 3 December 2020

Painter had not slept well until he heard from the solicitor that his client was indeed prepared to make a formal statement. Depending on how today went, Painter's sleep pattern might be about to recover. He had rehearsed everything with Ruth and just had to hope the interview went to plan. Things started well as he saw who the client was.

"For the benefit of the tape, the people present are Inspector Bill Painter, Dr Ruth Barnes, Albert Harris and Mr Dominic Fitzhugh, his solicitor. I have explained that Mr Harris will be interviewed under caution and that his replies may be presented in court."

Ruth then asked a series of questions.

"Albert, when we last met, I made it clear that you and your three friends could be facing the possibility of a very serious charge, that of murder. If convicted, you could be sentenced to spend many years in prison. However, murder is not the only possible charge, because you might be considered an accessory to murder which is much less serious. There's a clear understanding between us, your solicitor and anyone who listens to this tape that we believe that you were only an accessory to murder, not someone who should be charged with murder itself. I want to help you to get to that conclusion by exploring what we think your contribution was to this enterprise. Are you happy to discuss this?"

Albert looked towards Dominic for guidance. Painter's whole world stood still as he sat, holding his breath, waiting to hear if this case was going to finally come to fruition or collapse again.

After just a moment or two, which felt like a lifetime, Dominic nodded in reply, guiding his client to speak up.

"Yes, I am."

Painter hoped his exhalation had not been heard by the room or the tape. He relaxed as Ruth continued:

"We've spent a lot of time investigating this case. In summary, we think the two girls were the brains behind the scheme not you. Your mistake was to get mixed up in their plan. This is not all your fault."

Albert looked as if the weight of the world was beginning to lift from his shoulders.

"We know what the group has done apart from a few minor details. If you tell us those details, Inspector Painter here will also recommend that the judge is lenient towards you because you will have helped bring the case to a conclusion quickly. Are you ready to help the Inspector now and get a short sentence?"

Albert looked towards Dominic who nodded back.

"Yes, I am."

"Then let's start with Sir John; how did he come to be eating refreshments in the Rolls Royce you were driving?"

"It started after his wife banned pastries to go with the coffee at the board meeting because she said he was putting on too much weight. He grumbled to me as we drove along, saying that it wasn't just the food, he missed the experience of going back to his schooldays and eating what he called *tuck*. He then asked if I could get him some and keep it quiet from Lady Pilkington. I said I was happy to do that provided that he told me exactly the sort of food he was interested in. He explained that *tuck* varied from day to day at his school but might be a sticky bun, an iced bun or a piece of flapjack. I said I knew where to get those fresh and the deal was done. When he got out of the car, he gave me a fifty-pound note for my trouble plus a twenty to buy the first items. He swore me to keep it all secret. As he set off to go to his meeting, he seemed a happy and younger man."

Dominic raised a finger, indicating that he wanted to say something, but Ruth held up her hand and continued:

"To get this exactly correct for the tape, is it true to say then that the idea of you providing food items to Sir John was entirely his idea?"

"Yes, that's right."

Ruth looked to Dominic to see if that had addressed the point he wanted to make and the solicitor replied with a thumbs-up. Ruth consulted her notes and returned to the questioning.

"We then come to the date of Tuesday 18 August 2020 when 7 WhatsApp messages passed from Mandy, Louise, yourself, Kevin, Louise, you again and then Mandy. We can't read the actual messages, but will suggest in court that you were all agreeing a time to meet somewhere for Mandy to give the 3 poisoned food or drink items to the others; is that correct?"

"Yes, it is; we met in Nunhead cemetery."

"What form did the item intended for Sir John take? If it was a sticky bun, it would be pretty stale by the time he ate it on Monday 28 September, the day he was poisoned."

"Mandy gave a piece of Turkish delight to Louise and a gummy bear to Kevin. Mandy said she'd provide me with a suitable bun on the night before I was to give it to Sir John."

Dominic again raised a finger, but Ruth pressed on:

"Does that mean that Mandy added the poison to the food item intended for Sir John, not you?"

"Yes, that's right."

Dominic gave a thumbs-up showing that Ruth had got onto the tape precisely the point he wanted to make.

"Exactly what food item did Mandy give you and when did she deliver it?"

"It was a sticky bun with white icing. We met at Baker Street station on the night of Sunday 27 September and she passed it to me then."

"Did Sir John eat it all the next day?"

"Yes, he wolfed it down."

"Now think carefully about this next set of questions, Albert. What did you think when the suggestion was first made that your group of childhood friends should work as a team once again?"

"I thought it was a great idea. We'd had fun playing together as kids and forming a group to get things done. It was all a bit sad, us meeting up at the funeral of my granddad, so it seemed a good idea that something positive should come out of it."

"What was your first project?"

"We wanted to find out more about this Covid-19. We wanted to protect our elderly relatives and Evie. We looked up lots of articles on the Internet and discussed them."

"What was the mood of the group when the second death occurred?"

"The sadness at the loss of my granddad was still there when Kevin's mother Margaret died, but we also got a bit angry. She wasn't as old as Albert and should have had many years in front of her."

"What about the third death?"

"When Louise's father Peter died, we got even more angry. These were people doing their job during the pandemic but not being protected by their places of work or by the government."

"What about the fourth case?"

"The loss of Evie was tragic. She was our age. It showed that no-one was safe from the new virus. It seemed criminal that bosses were still not providing protection. We all got very angry and decided to get back at the managers."

"How did the group choose which managers to target?"

"Mandy said she could brew up a poison to make them all sick. She could get at Lord Yeast because she served him food. She said this was only fitting because his brewery was the one that employed her sister, Evie."

"How did the others respond to this?"

"We all said it would be fair to make him sick."

Dominic raised a finger again, but Ruth pressed on:

"Was the aim to make him sick or to kill him?"

"No-one mentioned killing anyone. I thought he'd just get the shits from the brew Mandy made."

Dominic again gave a thumbs-up to show that the tape now contained precisely the point he wanted to make.

"Which manager did the group choose next?"

"Kevin said that his boss was known to love gummy bears. Mandy said she could easily get her poison into one of those. When the group realised that this supermarket was the one that employed Kevin's mother Margaret, we all agreed it would be a fair punishment."

"What about the third manager?"

"Louise said it was obvious her boss fancied her. If she let him have his wicked way, she could reward him with some food. Once this became a habit, she could substitute something with poison in it. Mandy suggested Turkish delight as something that could be shared between lovers. The group all agreed this was fitting because the man worked for London Transport who employed Louise's father Peter as a bus driver."

"The last manager must have been Sir John."

"That's right. They were very keen to go after him once they worked out that his company owned the care home where my grandfather caught Covid and died. Mandy pushed me to think of a way for me to give him food or drink. When I told them that he'd recently asked me to get him *tuck* to eat in the car, they all celebrated. Someone said we had a full set; one manager representing each company with connections to the 4 relatives taken from us."

"Just one more question now, Albert. You gave Sir John the poisoned piece of *tuck*, dropped him at Mayfair and continued as normal for the rest of the day. What did you think when you heard he'd been taken to hospital?"

"I was a bit pleased that he was sick but worried that he needed to go to hospital. I wondered if Mandy had put too large a dose in the *tuck*."

"And what did you think when he died?"

"I was really shocked. If I could have gone back in

time, I'd never have agreed to give him the iced bun. I could see how Lady Pilkington was upset. I then realised that I'd probably lost the job I loved as well, because she wouldn't need a chauffeur any more."

"Did you discuss this with the group?"

"Yes, I did, but they were all happy with the outcome. They wanted to kill all 4 of these managers. I said I wanted nothing more to do with it, but Mandy told me to shut up, saying they had it coming to them."

Ruth looked at Painter and, receiving a nod, ended the interview.

"Thank you for coming in today, Albert. In my experience you'll soon feel better now that you've relieved yourself of the burden of all those secrets. To summarise, the information you've provided supports our idea that you're not someone who should be prosecuted for murder. For the benefit of the tape, this interview is now terminated."

Dominic had a quiet word with Painter in the corridor.

"Thank you for guiding my client today. Please do what you can to persuade the CPS and the judge to keep the punishment to a minimum."

"You know I can't anticipate exactly what the CPS will say, but you've had a good idea about what my recommendation will be. Thank you for getting in touch and I hope justice will be done for your client."

Dominic shook Painter's hand. He then turned and shook Ruth's hand vigorously as he thanked her for the expert questioning, before guiding Albert out of the building.

Painter and Ruth joined the others in the viewing room once Albert and Dominic had left.

"That was all very satisfactory. We now know that Mandy was the principal party and guiding mind for this enterprise. She had the most skin in the game because it was her sister who died. Mandy booked the bungalow at Peacehaven, prepared the poison and contaminated all 4 food items. She should go down for 25 years for murder. Louise was a secondary party. She was key to establishing the campaign, seduced her target and delivered the poisoned Turkish delight. She should get 20 years. Kevin is also a secondary party. He delivered the poisoned gummy bear. Three people had died by then so he can't claim that he didn't realise the poison was lethal. He should get 15 years. Finally, we have Albert. He was persuaded to use an existing request from Sir John to give him *tuck* as a means of delivering a poisoned iced bun. Since this was the first case, It's plausible that he didn't realise the outcome would be death, but that, on its own, is not a defence against murder because either death or serious harm is what's looked for. I think he'll be charged as an accessory to murder and might get 5-10 years. He's also been a great assistance to our case; indeed, a successful prosecution would have been impossible without him. The CPS will know this, so I hope they'll go for the lesser of the 5–10-year span. With good behaviour he could be out in 3 years. In contrast, Louise's beauty will wither while she's inside and she'll be middle aged before she gets out. I'm now off to put all of that into an email to our friends at the CPS."

∞

Thursday 10 December 2020

The days dragged on until Painter saw an email appear on his screen with the subject: **response from CPS re case 4172359.**

He quickly opened the message and held his breath as he read:

The statement and confession by Albert Harris have changed our assessment of this case. We now believe there is a reasonable chance of conviction and so authorise prosecution of all 4 suspects, 3 on counts of murder and one of accessory to murder. Our reasoning and suggested target penalties for the 4 are detailed below…

THE END

Postscript

It was time to pour his favourite and most expensive malt whisky into a glass and savour some excellent jazz. The fiery, peaty flavour of Lagavulin complemented Miles Davis' *Kind of Blue* perfectly.

He closed his eyes and let his brain take him back to where this had all started. He could see Evie and her younger sister Mandy playing with Louise in the garden. Albert and Kevin were there also; part of the group, but somewhat in the shadow of the brighter girls. The play became more animated and they slipped out through the gate into the verdant green of the cemetery, with evening sunlight slanting down through the trees. He could also visualise parents keeping a watching eye through the kitchen windows of the adjacent terraced houses. The picture was of an idyllic childhood; supportive families, good neighbours, friendly children, space to discover the world safely and all under the guiding wisdom of the local church vicar.

Painter normally dealt with lifelong crooks whose criminal tendencies were instilled by their family and ingrained by childhood training and neglect that failed to remove the grime and stains of their inadequate upbringing. Yet, the Fatal Five were law abiding, respectable kids from good, hard-working families. It just showed how citizens could be made to flip under the pressure of a final insult to their way of life. He was reminded of when he read *Lord of the Flies* in his own childhood.

While this perfect beginning should have set the children up for life, a quarter of a century later, a once in a lifetime pandemic rushed through to destroy their dreams. The virus brought illness and deaths of loved ones, including two parents, one grandparent and even one of the Fatal Five themselves. Politicians proved to be no match for Covid-19, allowing citizens to be overwhelmed and exploited. Even as the public congregated weekly on their doorsteps to clap for essential workers, those in charge were calculating how they could refuse to improve the working conditions of ordinary people once the crisis was over. Shocked by the duplicity of the current political class, Painter opened his eyes to now see revealed before him the fiery crucible that had created the Fatal Five.

Painter doubted whether the system would ever change, regardless of which political party was in power. Instead, was there a role for more agitation from those stuck in the lower sections of society? Should that agitation involve direct action? He could never endorse people taking the law into their own hands; we couldn't survive as a country with vigilantes running wild. Yet, under the influence of the malt and the mellow jazz he wondered

if the limited, targeted campaign run by the Fatal Five hadn't, just for once, allowed the little people to get their own back.